ICE CREAM WARS

A.E. RADLEY
EMMA STERNER-RADLEY

Heartsome Publishing

Reviews

We sincerely hope you'll enjoy reading Ice Cream Wars.

If you do, we would greatly appreciate a short review on your favourite book website.

Reviews are crucial for any author, and even just a line or two can make a huge difference.

ONE

Juliana's Morning

JULIANA MARTIN-SINCLAIR PARKED her grey Mercedes in the space marked *Reserved Parking - The Gelato Parlour*. She used the car's 360-degree camera to ensure it sat straight and precisely in the middle. Not until she was sure it was perfect did she exit the car and breathe in the morning air. It was chilly for late May, but then the town of Wilmsford was in Cheshire, not the tropics.

She buttoned her suit jacket and strode through the back door of what she thought of as her *gelateria*, despite everyone else in town calling it an "ice-cream shop". She sold high-quality Italian gelato and French sorbet, not sugary, chemical *ice cream* with more calories than flavour. Not that most of her clientele could tell the difference. Neither could Aaron Lewins, her one employee who only kept his position because he didn't mind Juliana being—she hesitated, not wanting to use the words "difficult and irritable," before deciding on "passionate and thorough."

Thinking about him made her start the day by searching him out to say good morning.

"Aaron? Where are you?"

"I'm out in the shop," he called. "I've prepped almost everything, just putting the tubs in the display case now."

Juliana passed her office. As she headed in his direction, she stroked her thick, black hair to make sure it hadn't been ruffled out of its ponytail. She stopped in horror when she entered the shop and saw Aaron placing the tubs of gelato and sorbet into the glass case.

"What are you doing?"

"Good morning, Juliana," he said, terribly cheerful. "I'm plonking the frozen treats down for our lucky future customers."

She set her jaw. "What have I told you about mixing the sorbets and gelatos?"

"Uh. Not to." He looked down at the tubs. "And I just did."

"Yes."

"Sorry. I was at a friend's birthday bash last night, guess I'm not quite awake."

He blinked his bloodshot eyes repeatedly, and Juliana had to wonder if he wasn't a tad hungover, too.

"I suppose that explains why you haven't colour-coordinated them either?"

"Uh. Yeah?" His smile was a little too close to relief for her liking.

"It *explains* it, Aaron; it doesn't *excuse* it. You need to stop partying every night and rolling in here like some form of zombie sloth. Rearrange them. Immediately."

"What? All of them?"

"No, just your favourite three. Yes, all of them."

In his defence, he didn't grumble or grimace. He took all the tubs out and placed the sorbets on the right and the gelatos on the left, ranging from the white ones to the darkest blackberry purples and chocolate browns.

She watched him as he worked, unable to move on to her next task until the nuisance had done his job correctly.

She threw a glance around to make sure he hadn't ruined anything else. No, it all looked spotless and flawless as expected. All the tiling, marble, and metal in white, black, and grey were shiny and dust-free. The counter gleamed and smelled of the lavender-scented cleaning spray. Even the expensive array of coffee-making devices shone in the morning sun. Her mouth watered at the thought of the day's first espresso.

Soon.

Aaron just had to use his single brain cell to decide if the vanilla pod sorbet was lighter in shade than the lemon one.

She could help him, of course, but if she did, he'd never learn. Also, she was paying him to get these things right, not to be window dressing. Not with that amount of body hair. Or that posture. Or that lime-green shirt with those navy trousers. Straight men's frequent lack of fashion sense never ceased to distress her. Could she force him to go home and change? She really had to implement a Gelato Parlour uniform. For Aaron, of course. No one was touching her Savile Row suits.

He put the final tub down and faced her. "There. I'm… wait, why are you looking at me like that. You okay? Am I okay? Do I have cherry-wine gelato in my beard again?"

She shifted back into work mode. "No. I was simply wondering if you had learned your lesson. However, no one can hope for that much. Now, move on to your next task."

"Aye, aye, general," he mumbled under his breath.

"What was that?"

"Nothing," he squeaked. "I just said I'd get right to it."

He rushed out, and Juliana was left standing there smiling to herself.

General? she thought. *Not a bad title to be given on a regular Tuesday morning. That deserves an espresso.*

TWO

Cherry's Morning

____

RIDING the ice cream trike wasn't quite the same as riding a normal bike as Cherry Hawkins had hoped it would be. The trike was heavy and, yes, a little unwieldy, but also tremendous fun.

She'd saved up and even borrowed some money from her mum in order to purchase the trike. It had one wheel at the back and two at the front. In between the front wheels was a large freezer unit that Cherry had stuffed with as much frozen ice cream product as she could.

Emblazoned on the side of the freezer was her company logo and name—"Cherry on Top"—in bright pinks and fresh creams.

Ever since she was a child, she had wanted to be involved in the ice cream business. Preferably eating it, possibly making it, maybe selling it. She didn't care too much as long as it involved her favourite sugary treat.

In high school, she'd formulated a business plan and come up with the name; in university, she'd studied business and marketing in order to bring her one step closer to her dream. She'd saved every penny from her part-time jobs at uni and couldn't believe the day had finally come that she could call herself a self-employed ice cream seller.

The trike was a stroke of genius. She'd seen one when she was visiting the beach a couple of years earlier. An elderly man had ridden past her after having packed up for the day. She'd seen his trike, realised he was selling ice cream, and then proceeded to run after him—no easy feat in the scorching summer temperatures and flip flops.

He'd eventually noticed her and stopped, apologetically saying that he'd run out of ice cream to sell. She'd gazed at the trike in awe; it was exactly what she needed, the perfect way to start trading without having to take out a huge business loan. The man had given her the details of a custom trike production company in Derbyshire, and Cherry had coveted her own trike ever since.

She'd eventually saved enough for a down payment and had worked with the company to make her very own ice cream trike. She frequently visited the factory to watch its production move forward, and when she'd picked it up a week ago, she couldn't believe her dreams were finally becoming a reality.

She stood up, balancing on the pedals and enjoying

the wind in her hair. She hoped that no one was going to walk in front of her any time soon. Steering was hard and stopping was impossible. The frontloaded weight of the ice cream meant that she was essentially along for the ride, a ride that was gradually increasing in speed.

But Cherry wasn't worried. Things generally worked out.

She looked at the piece of paper she gripped in her hand. It had taken a lot of paperwork and even more back and forth with the council, but she'd eventually managed to obtain a trading permit.

The council weren't too keen on the idea of Cherry cycling around the posh town of Wilmsford like most trike sellers would. They preferred to give her a permit for a fixed location.

At first, she'd been disappointed at not being able to wind her way through the streets, but since taking the fully loaded trike for a ride, she realised it was for the best. If someone did want to flag her down for an ice cream, she doubted she'd be able to stop.

She attempted to read the permit again. It fluttered manically in her hand as the wind caught it. As were most things from the council, the permit was very specific about where she was to park up her bike and be allowed to trade. Luckily, she'd been granted a spot in the busiest part of the main road through town, right in the middle of the large, pedestrianised area surrounded by shops.

She gently applied the handbrakes. Relief swept through her when she actually managed to slow down. After a few tiny adjustments of the handlebars and some heavy squeezing of the brake levers, Cherry came to a stop. She studied the permit and then scanned the pedestrianised area.

"In between the fountain and the oak tree, next to the lamppost. This is it," she said to herself.

She checked the permit again. It showed a map of the area with a little red square denoting her trading space.

"Yep, this is it. Home!"

She kicked down the trike stand and jumped off the pedals.

The high street was deserted. She heard the distant sounds of a few shops opening and preparing for the business day ahead.

Cherry unclipped the umbrella from the trike and opened it up, placing the large parasol in the clamps on the handlebar. It wasn't quite warm enough to need the cover, but she'd paid extra for the umbrella and she was bloody well going to use it.

She slid out an A-board from beneath the freezer, unfolded it, and propped it on the ground. She tilted her head and eyed it for a moment, wondering if it was facing the best direction.

After a few minutes of fractionally moving it to the left and then the right, she left it alone. She was a little nervous and a lot excited. Her first day was about to start—the culmination of years of dreaming and planning.

She put a smile on and paced around the bike, eager for her first customer.

THREE

A Bicycle Buffoon Ruins the Day

JULIANA STOOD up and stretched her neck, moaning softly as something popped and some of the stiffness eased. She had to stop eating her lunch while going over the accounts. That time should be used to sit up straight or move about to avoid serious injuries. However, the thought of wasting time by not working as she ate was worse than the crick in her neck.

Adjusting her shirt collar, she walked out into the shop to relieve Aaron for his lunch break. When she got there, she found the place strangely deserted. The afternoon had turned sunny, and so she expected to find her usual customer base of well-to-do mothers drinking lattes while their offspring wailed about the lack of chocolate sauce on their frozen treats. Instead, there was only a stressed woman spilling her sorbet over some paperwork and an eccentric author type wedged in his corner, nursing a cup of tea over his battered laptop.

Juliana turned to Aaron. "What have you done with all my customers?"

"Huh?"

"Don't say 'huh?' like that. Where is everyone?"

"Oh. Um." Just above his beard, pink coloured his cheeks. "I don't think you'll like the answer."

"I think I'll like a lack of answer even less," she all but hissed.

"All the m-mums wanted to try the new place," he stuttered. "I m-mean, the kids wanted the ice cream, but the mums fancied the novelty of the set-up, I think. Even if that means they can't get their coffee hit right away."

Juliana held up a hand. "Stop. You're babbling. Explain properly."

Before he had time to answer, a jovial female voice rang out, "Get your ice cream! Fresh and yummy! I'm almost out of the caramel-marshmallow swirl, so you better hurry!"

Juliana stared in the direction of the shouting. In the pedestrian area right outside her shop stood a woman with a bicycle, a childish umbrella, and some sort of large cooling device. Around her were women in designer jeans and their toddlers in smaller designer jeans.

Juliana had found her missing customers.

She glared at the woman, who was now waving her hands for attention and shouting about the brownie flavour being sold out.

"What is that ginger nut doing with my customers?" Juliana said in a low voice.

Aaron perked up. "Ginger nut? Does she sell biscuits, too?"

"No, you fool. Ginger was in reference to her hair colour while the nut part came from her vigorous body language and infernal shouting."

"Isn't her hair too light to be ginger? Isn't that like, what do they call it, raspberry blonde?"

Strawberry blonde, she internally corrected him. Out loud she said, "Focus, Aaron. What. Is. She. Doing?"

"Selling ice cream."

"I can see that, you twit. I meant why is she doing it on the street right across from my gelateria?"

"I don't know."

"You didn't go out there and ask her?"

"Nope. Should I have?"

Juliana closed her eyes and counted to ten. "Never mind. I'll do it myself."

She rushed out, her heeled boots pounding the small distance between her respectable business and this woman's my-little-ice-cream-shop toy bike.

When she was right in front of the redhead, Juliana raked her eyes over her in disbelief. She was wearing fabric shoes, tight black leggings, and a large, unzipped yellow anorak over what was probably a T-shirt. She was in great shape—no doubt from wasting her time cycling around on that silly contraption—and appeared to be in her mid-twenties. This meant Juliana had more than ten years on this woman, not that she'd need them to add to her superiority over this tasteless pest.

Juliana placed her hands on her hips with slow, studied refinement and in a clear voice said, "Good afternoon."

The woman turned to her with a dazzling, customer-service smile. "Hi there! Fancy an ice cream? You look like you'd enjoy the maple walnut."

"I look like I'd what?" Juliana snarled. "Why on earth would *I* come to *you* for an ice cream?"

One of the customers, who was clearly eavesdropping and knew very well who Juliana was, gasped.

The bicycle buffoon, however, only looked politely surprised. "Because that's what I sell? Sorry, I don't have any posh coffees. People have been asking for them, but as you can see, ice cream is all I've got room for."

"Oh, really? Well. I don't have that problem. You see, I have what we call a *shop*. In which I sell not only coffees but also quality gelato and sorbet." Juliana pointed back to the Gelato Parlour. "So, no, I do not need your frozen sugar bombs. What I need is for you to pedal your monstrosity away before I call the council about you cluttering up the town centre."

The redhead leaned on her handlebars and squinted

over at the Gelato Parlour. "Whoa. That place sells ice cream? It looks too... serious and dull for that. I thought it sold insurance or something."

Juliana clenched her hands into fists. "If you don't move along presently, I *will* alert the council."

"Go ahead. They'll tell you that I have a permit," the other woman replied, patting the pocket of her over-sized anorak. "Since we're neighbours, I should introduce myself. I'm Cherry, as in 'Cherry On Top'," she said, pointing to the sign. "I assume your name isn't 'Gelato' or 'Parlour'? Snazzy business name, by the way. Could've used some more imagination, but never mind, eh?"

Cherry's smile wasn't mocking. It looked more like a light-hearted, sweet, teasing thing, which made her eyes twinkle in the sunlight.

Juliana hated it beyond all measure.

"So. You have a permit, do you? We'll see about that. I happen to know Colin Greene, who is in charge of business permits. I think I'll pay him a visit at the council office."

Juliana didn't mention that she couldn't stand the smarmy and borderline-corrupt Colin Greene, nor that he wasn't very fond of her either. Cherry didn't need to know that.

"Okey-dokey. Go ahead. Tell him if he wants some ice cream, I'll give him a discount on whatever I haven't already sold out," Cherry said with another smile.

Juliana snorted and turned on her heels. She

stormed towards the parking lot and her Mercedes, already planning how she would lay out her case for having Cherry decapitated—or at least run out of Wilmsford!

Entering the Dragon's Lair

THE CRAZY WOMAN'S outburst had caused a lot of shoppers to disperse. If Cherry hadn't been on the other end of said outburst, she probably would've run away as well. That eruption aside, it had been a good day. The fine people of Wilmsford seemed to enjoy the new flavours Cherry was carrying. She may have just been a bike, a freezer, and an umbrella, but that hadn't stopped her from nearly selling out.

She looked at the Gelato Parlour and shook her head. She honestly hadn't noticed the slick, black-and-chrome shopfront. Of course, she knew *something* was there. She hadn't thought she was set up next to a wasteland, but she'd never given the building a second look. The signage looked dull, and the windows were practically blacked out.

It was kind of invisible.

The rude owner had stormed up the street, presumably to go and complain to the council as she had promised. Cherry glanced around the high street. There were a few people around, but they all seemed to be in a hurry. Not likely customers for her.

It was the perfect opportunity to lock up and go and check out the supposed competition. She locked the freezer and put the chain on her trike, not wanting anyone to cycle off with her entire business.

She walked over to the parlour's entrance and had a look at the menu in the glass cabinet by the door. She shook her head, marvelling that she had stood there all morning and had no idea there was a gelateria right next to her.

The bonkers woman hadn't been exaggerating. She really did sell gelato, sorbet, and coffees. Lots and lots of coffees. That probably explained her outburst, seeing as she was ninety percent caffeine.

Cherry pushed on the door and stepped inside. Classical music played softly in the background. The two customers looked up at her, scowled slightly at the disturbance, then continued to work.

Cherry closed the door behind her and looked around the inside of the parlour. It was very… sterile.

"Hi, can I help you?" A hipster-looking guy was staring at her suspiciously from behind the counter.

Cherry put on a smile and walked over the glass display cabinets.

"Hi, I'm Cherry. From Cherry on Top outside. Thought I'd come and introduce myself."

She held up a hand, and he shook it.

"I'm Aaron. Welcome to the Gelato Parlour."

"Original name," Cherry quipped.

She looked inside the cabinets at all the tubs of frozen product, lined up by colour, with neat little plastic signs stabbed into each of them. The uninspiring name seemed to extend to the flavours as well.

"Lemon?" she asked. "Not even 'lemon drop'?"

"Juliana doesn't like a lot of the common names," Aaron explained.

"Juliana? Was that who came storming out of here, all fire in her eyes?"

"Yep. She's my boss."

Cherry winced. "Ouch. My condolences."

"She's okay." Aaron shrugged. Judging by his nervous shifting from foot to foot and the way his eyes continually snapped up to door as if he expected the arrival of Satan himself, Juliana was *not* okay.

Cherry walked toward the next display case and nodded as she took in the neat, orderly sorbets. She took a couple of steps back and read the full menu, written in silver calligraphy on a blackboard above the counter.

"I don't see her issue," she declared. "We're completely different. I sell ice cream and fun. She sells coffee, gelato, sorbets, and… darkness."

Aaron smiled a little. It vanished in a flash, though, as one of the customers dropped a spoon. The loud clatter had him jumping out of his skin.

"Are you okay?" Cherry asked.

He nodded quickly. Too quickly. "Yep. Fine. Just… are you leaving soon? It's just, if Juliana sees you in here, and me talking to you…"

"She'll be mad?" Cherry guessed.

"Yeah. She's not so bad when everything is calm. When she gets stressed, though…" He visibly swallowed.

"I don't want to get you in trouble, I only wanted to see what you guys did. I don't want to take any business away from anyone, but we're different, you know?" She gestured around the space. "You have a different… vibe."

"Juliana won't see that," Aaron predicted.

"Well, then she'll have to take it up with the council. I asked for a permit fair and square, and that's what I have. We might as well be friends rather than enemies. Right, neighbour?" Cherry grinned at him.

Aaron grimaced. "I don't mind you being there. I think your bike is cute."

"It's a trike, and it's bloody adorable," Cherry corrected with a large grin.

Aaron chuckled and nodded in agreement before he let out a big sigh. "But Juliana, she's not big on compromise. Or change. Or competitors. Or cute trikes." He looked apologetic, and Cherry knew it was the face of someone who was unfortunately caught in the middle.

She shrugged her shoulders. "Never mind, she'll get used to me. We'll all be friends soon enough."

Aaron laughed nervously. "Sure, okay."

"See you around, neighbour." She offered him a friendly wave and started to leave. As she put her hand on the door handle, a woman sat at a nearby table looked up.

"Do you have Chunky Monkey?"

"Sure do," Cherry confirmed.

"In a cone?"

"Sure, waffle or wafer?"

The woman's eyes lit up, and she started to gather her belongings. Cherry looked at Aaron regretfully as she led the way to her trike. It wasn't her fault she had what people wanted.

FIVE

Only Family Can Understand

Juliana marched out of the council building and got in her Mercedes, slamming the door shut. She smoothed a crease in her skirt, but it wouldn't stay flat. Not even that was going right today. She growled in frustration. How dare that ice-cream hippie colonise the area outside her gelateria? And how dare that excuse for a councillor Colin Greene give her permission to do so?

Juliana needed to vent. But to whom? Aaron would be as much use as a sounding board as a headache pill in a leper colony. It struck her who she needed to call. Only another Martin-Sinclair would understand the depth of this affront, and not waste time on small talk or explanations.

She retrieved her phone from her handbag and called her brother.

"Eduardo Martin-Sinclair speaking," he answered quickly, as always.

"I need to talk to you."

"Ah, Juliana. What can I do for my darling little sister?"

"I need you to strangle Colin Greene."

"Oh, I'm sure someone would have done that long ago if it hadn't been exceedingly illegal."

Juliana thumped her head back against the leather headrest. "Why? People kill toads all the time, and they're not sent to jail."

"Sadly, this toad masquerades as a human and is therefore protected by the law. What has he done now?"

Juliana told him all about Cherry with her permit and her ridiculous bicycle. She finished with how she had stormed into Colin's office a few minutes ago to have him calmly claim that there was nothing he could do. "So, to sum it all up, that vile little man with his equally vile smirk told me that there were no other pitches to give to what he called 'that enterprising girl'. Such rubbish!"

"Agreed," Eduardo said. "Wilmsford's town centre is full of quaint, cosy spots under trees and by benches which he could have designated in her permit. The gormless twit *chose* to place her outside your gelateria. Couldn't he see your issue with that?"

"He said he saw no problem with it, but you and I both know that he did. It's clear that he hates all Martin-Sinclairs—ever since he worked for papá and was told a few truths about his lack of intelligence, at least. Obviously making my life harder when he signed off on this was a bonus for him."

"Juliana, you can't blame all of that on papá. You have antagonised Colin the Toad on several occasions."

She frowned. "Well, I've been forced to do so because Colin is a blithering simpleton who can't do his job. Not to mention a chauvinistic annoyance who is prone to corruption."

"True," Eduardo said.

Juliana could hear papers being shuffled and a phone ringing in the background. Her brother worked in the financial sector in London and was clearly busy. She should have thought about that before calling.

She rubbed her forehead, careful not to wipe away any makeup. "I apologise if this was a bad time to call, Eduardo. I just had to talk to someone who would understand."

"It's fine. I would be furious in your situation, too. In fact, I'm furious despite having nothing to do with this mess. I do have a meeting I need to prepare for soon, though." There was more shuffling of papers before he added, "Before I go, putting Colin and the useless council aside, what about the young woman? This Cheri?"

"It's *Cherry*, Cherry Hawkins. I know, apparently fruits can be names now."

"Right, this Cherry. Could you talk to her? Ask her to keep pressuring Colin for a more appropriate parking spot? Surely the competition can't be good for her either."

Juliana thought back to the annoyingly pretty, fresh-faced thing who squinted at her beloved gelateria and said it looked too dull to sell ice creams. "She doesn't seem to see us as competitors."

"Well, that's ridiculous," Eduardo said with indignation.

"I know!"

"What is wrong with people these days? You should see some of the twentysomethings I have to work with here. Head in the sky and entitlement streaming out of their unhearing ears."

"Precisely! That's what this ginger-haired sugar rat is like!"

"You need to do something about this, Juliana. You can't let the twentysomethings and the toads of this world set the rules."

She took a firm grip of her steering wheel. "Don't worry. I won't."

A smile tugged at the corner of her lips as her mind kicked into a new gear. Maybe there was a way to drive Cherry away without going through official channels.

"All is fair in love and war," she muttered, half lost in thought.

"Yes, and if this is a war, I know you will be the conquering force."

She was truly smiling now as her plan solidified and

gleamed in her mind's eye. "Oh, you can count on it, brother dear."

SIX

Swimming with the Fish (Heads)

CHERRY BALANCED on the pedals of her trike and enjoyed picking up speed from the top of the hill. The wind whipped through her hair and her anorak flapped loudly behind her, making her feel like Supergirl. She'd gotten up extra early that morning to try to figure out a way to pack even more ice cream into the trike's freezer.

Getting up at six in the morning wasn't Cherry's idea of fun. However, she knew she would need the extra time to go through the previous day's sales and decide what to take with her that morning. The industrial freezer in her garage was full of flavours, and she could only fit around a tenth of her inventory into the portable freezer on the trike.

The previous day had gone spectacularly, better than she could have imagined, and now she had an idea of what Wilmsford's ice-cream-adoring public were after. It had taken her an hour to decide what to take with her and how to cram it into the smaller freezer. Eventually she was happy with what she had accomplished and cycled her way into town.

It was another glorious morning. The streets were empty, the birds were singing, and the sun was starting to shine. Not to mention that there was something beautiful and freeing about careening to work on an ice cream trike.

She still hadn't quite gotten the hang of controlling the heavy vehicle, so at this point she was just along for the ride. The good thing about the hard work of cycling to and from the high street everyday was that she definitely earned an ice cream treat.

She applied her brakes a little, though, as she got closer to her pitch. Her eyes widened. Something was terrible, horribly wrong.

The brakes screeched as she came to a complete stop a few meters away from her destination. She stared in horror. She looked around to see if anyone was there to share in her outrage before she looked again.

Her pitch was occupied by an enormous industrial waste bin, which was overflowing with bags of smelly garbage.

"What the hell?"

She kicked down the trike stand and walked over to get a closer look. The smell was atrocious, like rotting fish and spoilt milk. Cherry walked around it, wondering why on earth it was in the middle of the high street. What kind of person would leave a large, smelly bin there?

She paused. An uninspiring logo was stuck to one side of the container.

"I'll kill her," Cherry mumbled.

She spun round and stormed towards the Gelato Parlour. They weren't open for business yet, but the door was unlocked so Cherry shoved it open.

"Good morning," said the espresso-sipping lunatic from behind the counter.

"What have you done?" Cherry demanded.

"I've no idea what you're talking about. I'm Juliana, by the way. Juliana Martin-Sinclair."

"I know, and I don't care. Move your bin, right now!"

"And you are?" Juliana asked sweetly.

"You know who I am. I introduced myself before you strutted off to the council to get me thrown out of town. Now, why is your bin in my pitch?" Cherry folded her arms and stared at her.

Juliana still wore a butter-wouldn't-melt smile as she turned to peer out of the tinted glass. "Oh, yes, that. Aaron was moving it last night so it could be emptied. The area is pedestrianised, so we have to take it across the street to the pickup point. Sadly, the wheels snapped. It's impossible to move." She took another sip from her stupid, tiny cup. "Someone is coming to get it, though I can't tell you when that might be. You know what these service providers are like."

Cherry unfolded her arms and clenched her fists by her sides. Juliana didn't look sorry in the slightest. In fact, she looked pleased with herself as she blinked those annoyingly pretty brown eyes. Far too pleased.

"Why does it smell of fish? Do you do some kind of salmon sorbet that I didn't know about?" she asked.

"Fish?" Juliana made a big deal of appearing confused. "I'm afraid I don't know why it smells of fish. Maybe someone saw an abandoned bin and took advantage of it?"

Cherry knew she wasn't going to get much further talking to Juliana. She let out a frustrated sigh and marched towards the exit.

"Have a lovely day, dear," Juliana called after her.

"Bite me," Cherry mumbled under her breath.

She walked straight over to the bin, took a deep breath and held it in while pushing the big stink bomb with all her might. It didn't budge. She turned around and pushed her back up to the cold metal and tried again, pushing with everything she had.

Nothing.

She let out the breath and winced at the smell that immediately invaded her nostrils. She walked around the bin. One side was up on wheels, the other was flush against the ground with both wheels completely missing. She crouched down to see if the apparently snapped wheels were underneath.

They weren't.

"By the way!"

Cherry slowly turned to stare at Juliana, who was standing in the doorway to her shop, still holding her espresso.

"Yes?" she gritted out.

"Traders must stay within the location designated on their permit, no matter what. Ignoring your permit conditions could land you with an enormous fine, or even risk voiding your permit altogether." Another dainty sip of coffee. "Just thought I'd let you know, in case you thought you might set up elsewhere. Wouldn't want someone to report you and get you a nasty fine."

"Yes, that would be awful," Cherry agreed sarcastically.

Juliana ruffled her elegant nose at the smell from the bin. "I suspect that will get worse as the sun gets hotter. You might want to write today off and go home, dear."

Cherry watched Juliana go back into the Gelato Parlour and shook her head. If this force of nature of a woman wanted to go to war, so be it.

SEVEN

Triumph

Juliana glided back into her office with satisfaction humming through every part of her. She placed the espresso cup down on its saucer on her desk. Next to the saucer was a clean sheet of paper which was protecting the mahogany from the dirty objects laying atop it: two bin wheels, some screws, and a newly purchased screwdriver.

She gave the screwdriver a pleased little pat and sniggered under her breath, then sat down to get on with her paperwork. Admittedly, it was hard to focus with the image of Cherry's outraged cheeks turning redder than her hair dancing across her mind. Juliana wondered if the sugar rat was going to set up her ridiculous ice cream bicycle in the next town over or simply give up the venture altogether. Not that it mattered. All that mattered was that everything was back to normal. Everything was under her control again.

The clock in her office struck twelve. Juliana got up, checked the pressed crease on her suit trousers, and headed out to the shop to tell Aaron he could take his lunch break. As she did, she happened to cast a glance out through the window and saw that the tacky bicycle, with its exceedingly tacky umbrella and even tackier owner, was still there.

"Hm."

"What's that, boss?" Aaron asked while giving change to a customer.

Juliana smiled at the departing customer before she answered him. "The bicycle buffoon is still there."

"Yeah," he grumbled.

Juliana knew that his disapproval didn't come from Cherry still being on her pitch. In fact, she suspected he quite liked her. Whatever minor grumpiness he dared show came from the fact that Juliana had roped him into helping her move and disable the bin. She ignored his pouting and let her gaze linger on Cherry instead.

The woman had just taken off her oversized eyesore of a raincoat and now tried to coax customers to buy ice cream, despite the bin stink, while wearing a much more flattering and professionally fitted black T-shirt.

A young man took a few unsure steps towards the bicycle and its handwritten menu of flavours.

Juliana tapped her fingers against the counter. "I have to admit that I'm somewhat impressed. She didn't give up. Or cause a fuss. She's got both backbone and a solid work ethic."

"Uh-huh," Aaron muttered.

"Still. It's only a matter of time. She can't keep selling food by that foul-smelling bin."

The man who had dared approach Cherry suddenly backed away while wafting the air by his nose, proving Juliana's point.

"I'll go to lunch, then," Aaron said, pulling her out of her reverie.

"What? Oh yes, of course. Don't come back late."

If he glared at her as he left, which she knew he often did, Juliana missed it. She was too busy enjoying the glow of satisfaction as Cherry's would-be customer fled the bin smell and headed right to the Gelato Parlour instead.

"Good afternoon," she greeted as he entered the shop.

Juliana was heading to the bank to deposit the day's takings before they closed. The early evening was balmy and scented with flowers. Summer was definitely coming to Wilmsford. As she passed Cherry's spot, she was shocked to find not only that Cherry was still there, but that her bin *wasn't*. She halted mid-step.

Cherry had clearly noticed her falter because she turned from fiddling with her umbrella and leaned confidently against her handlebars while giving Juliana a roguish grin.

"Hi there."

"Hello," Juliana replied.

"Your bin's gone."

"I… I can see that. What have you done with it?"

"Me? Nothing. The bin company came to pick it up like you said."

"They did? But I didn't—" She stopped herself from saying that she hadn't contacted them just in time.

"Didn't think they'd come get it right away?" Cherry said with mock innocence. "Oh, they were very helpful when I chased them for you. It seems the email you sent them didn't arrive. Probably got lost in the ether, right?"

Juliana opened her mouth. Then closed it. Then got herself together. "Yes, it must have ended up in their spam filter."

"Yeah, of course. Tragic. Anyway, the bin is being fixed as we speak." Cherry stood to her full height before grinning wider and adding, "You're welcome."

There was no way in hell Juliana was going to say thank you. There was no way in hell she was going to say anything to that wicked smile and those gleaming, triumphant eyes.

Instead, she sniffed with disdain in Cherry's direction and headed towards the bank with as much composure as she could muster. She wasn't sure, but as she walked away, she thought she might've heard a quiet chuckling from that cursed bicycle buffoon.

EIGHT

Settling In

____

CHERRY RUSHED BACK from the public toilets. Being her own boss was great, but the role was not without its downsides. Not having someone to take over when nature called was definitely one of them. Luckily, Wilmsford had a set of not-too-shabby public toilets a mere three-minute walk away from her pitch.

At first, she'd worried how many customers she was missing out on every time she took a ten-minute break away from the trike, but she was selling out of ice cream each and every day, so she quickly realised it wasn't an issue.

It had been a week since she first set up, and it seemed that word about her was spreading already. Every day someone new popped by and told her that a friend had told them to try a certain flavour. She even had regulars, mainly mums who wanted to keep their kids quiet on the way home from school.

She'd figured out the best way to pack her freezer with as much ice cream as possible, even if it was sometimes slightly over the recommended weight limit. Her thermometer told her that the ice cream was still at the optimum temperature, which was her main concern. So what if her morning cycles were getting slower and slower as she made the trike heavier? At least of an evening she flew home with barely a scoop of ice cream left.

She rounded the corner from the public toilets and was now in view of the trike. No one seemed to be hanging around, which was good.

As her first seven days of trading had gone on, she'd tweaked her business operations, from stock, to pricing, to cone choices, to toilet break times. She was pretty impressed, even if she did say so herself. Her business dreams were becoming a reality, and she was actually successful. She'd always hoped for this, but she hadn't assumed it would happen so quickly.

Even Juliana seemed to have given up trying to upset her. Their turf war had fizzled out as abruptly as it had started. At least, Cherry hoped that was the case. She hoped Juliana wasn't cultivating a much bigger, much smellier bin.

She unlocked the freezer and removed her home-made sign that said 'Be Back Soon'.

"Ice cream!" she shouted. "Selling out fast, get it while it's in stock. All the best flavours, never seen before in Wilmsford!"

Cherry pitied the local shoppers. They had clearly only had boring, grown-up gelato flavours in the past. Watching their eyes light up at a flavourful ice cream was such a delight.

"There she is, Wilmsford's newest trader."

Cherry smiled at Colin Greene, the councillor she'd been dealing with to get her permit. "Hello, Mr Greene."

"I keep telling you, Colin is fine." He looked up at the trike parasol and pointed a finger. "Cute."

"Thank you. Would you like an ice cream? On the house, of course."

"Don't mind if I do. Just a small one, though." He patted his stomach. "Got to watch the weight."

Cherry opened the freezer and quickly made up a chocolate chip and mint ice cream in a waffle cone. She prided herself on being able to predict someone's flavour palette by just looking at them.

"Everything going well?" he asked. "Any issues?"

Cherry hated it when people asked questions that required different replies back to back.

"Everything is going brilliantly, unless you're here to tell me off?" She winked and handed him the cone. "On the house."

"Ooh, chocolate." He eagerly took the cone. "No, I'm not here to tell you off, just seeing how you are settling in. I like to check up on our traders."

Cherry doubted that. Colin Greene didn't seem like a man who did anything unless it benefitted him. Not that she had any personal gripes with him, just that she knew the sort. There was something slimy about him. He'd been completely uninterested in her permit application when she had spoken to him on the phone. However, when she'd gone to the office in person, his entire persona had changed. He'd pulled out a chair for her to sit in, offered her a hot drink, and even claimed to move her application to the top of the pile.

Cherry wasn't a stranger to men flirting with her or offering things to get into her good graces. She didn't think of herself as wildly attractive, but she knew she could be considered cute. Men like Colin certainly seemed to think so.

She was careful not to encourage them, they were most definitely barking up the wrong tree. But in the case of Colin Greene, she'd been polite and friendly in order to get her permit. There was no need to make an enemy out of the man who could literally make or break her career.

He took a bite of the ice cream and rolled his eyes in happiness.

"Mint. I love mint," he declared.

Cherry smiled, enjoying the feeling of getting her prediction spot on once more.

He jovially prodded her shoulder. "You're going to be terrible for my waistline, I can see it now!"

NINE

Rumour Has It...

____

JULIANA LINGERED in the corner of her shop, near the windows. This allowed her to not only see out but also to stay hidden from anyone who might try to peer in through the tinted glass. It was imperative that she kept an eye on Cherry and Colin the Toad out there. She had checked that no one from inside the shop was watching her keeping vigil. She had even taken precautions by holding a duster so she could pretend to be cleaning if they glanced over. This, however, might be overkill when there were only three customers and they were all preoccupied with their laptops and phones.

Three customers at peak time. Disastrous. Thank goodness for her takeaway coffees or the business she loved and had devoted her life to for the past twelve years would have to close down.

A cough from behind her made her jump.

"Sorry to scare you," Aaron whispered. "I was just wondering what you're doing?"

"I'm watching your favourite sugar peddler give Colin Greene a free ice cream. They also seem to be having an *intimate* chat," she whispered back with venom dripping from every word.

"Okay. Um, no offence, but… do you know that it looks a bit peculiar that you're hiding in this corner and staring at Cherry?"

"I am not," she hissed as loudly as she dared.

He looked genuinely perplexed. "Not what? Hiding or staring at Cherry?"

"Oh, do be quiet! Go serve the customers."

"They don't want anything else, Juliana. I asked."

"Then go dust the counter. Just go away," she hissed, this time a little too loudly, as one of the customers peered over but soon looked down at his phone again.

Aaron shrugged and walked away.

Juliana returned her focus to Cherry and Colin and gasped at what she saw. He was caressing Cherry's shoulder! She had actually let him touch her—and given him ice cream without taking payment! To make things worse, she kept smiling that annoyingly pretty smile of hers at him. There could be no doubt that this infuriating woman was playing dirty by buying the toad's favour.

That was both annoying and unsurprising, considering that Juliana had finally heard back about her formal complaint, the one she had lodged four days ago, that very morning. The email from the council had been waiting in her inbox to dash all her dreams by claiming that both Colin and Cherry were in the right while she was thoroughly in the wrong. The council wasn't going to rule in her favour no matter how much she complained. She was on her own against a world gone mad.

She squeezed the duster in her hand and decided to return to playing as dirty as Cherry was doing. This time she'd think up something that Cherry couldn't fix with a simple phone call, as in the case of the bin. She released her vice-like grip on the duster as the solution came to her.

At the moment, word of mouth was helping Cherry. Well. She would have to learn, like Juliana had early on in her career, that word of mouth could very quickly turn into nasty, unfounded rumours.

People love to lift someone up just to drag them down into the mud the next day, she thought with disgust. She remembered the lies that had spread about her and her female employee the second Wilmsford found out that Juliana was a lesbian.

Shaking off her discomfort, she went to the bathroom to check her make-up and clothes while she deliberated her approach. Then she picked up her handbag, told Aaron she'd be back soon, and headed down the road. She rushed past Cherry, who was thankfully busy with a customer—a real, paying one, not the toad.

Soon she found the person who would unwittingly help her solve her problem, dear old Herbert. He had a stall selling flowers at the start of the pedestrianised area and had been there for the past forty years, according to his own math.

"Well, hello there, Ms Martin-Sinclair! Fancy seeing you at this end of the high street."

"Hello, Herbert. How are you?"

"Aches and pains, but I'll live. How are your parents?"

"They're both well. In fact…" Juliana improvised, "I'm here to buy a nice bouquet for my mother. She deserves a treat."

Herbert smiled, showing his woeful lack of front teeth. "Why, how lovely of you!"

"I try my best," she said, only slightly guilty over involving her mother in this ploy. After all, she would get some flowers out of the deal. Furthermore, Juliana knew both her parents would approve of her doing whatever necessary to protect both her business and her mental equilibrium.

"How about these?" Herbert said, holding up a bouquet of mainly pink and white flowers.

"Perfect," she agreed.

While he wrapped them up for her and she fished her wallet out of her handbag, she said, "By the way, have you tried the ice cream that the precious young woman on the bicycle sells?"

"You mean Cherry and her trike? Oh, aye, she

convinced me to try a scoop of something called Coconut Dream. While I'm not one for these new fangled treats, that one was scrummy!"

Juliana tried to look neutral. "Yes, her recipes are really something. You know, it's quite impressive that she manages to keep her products cold and hygienic in that small, cheap-looking icebox all day. Especially as it seems quite overfilled."

His eyebrows knitted together. "Hm. Yes, I s'pose so."

"Particularly as I hear she makes these dairy products in her own kitchen and so may not put the necessary preservatives in them. Then it must be essential for the ice cream to be handled properly, I should think." She gave him a smile and the money for the flowers. "Of course, I wouldn't know the process, what with my award-winning suppliers and industrial, safety-certified freezers."

"I dare say you've got a point there," Herbert replied, now looking more pensive than she'd ever seen him.

"Mm. After all, I'd hate for anyone to become ill. Could you imagine one of the delicate children who often frequent her... little setup... coming down with stomach upsets and perhaps even catching something worse?"

His eyes went wide. "What? You mean like getting worms or somethin' like that?"

She was really taking liberties now and was fully

aware that someone less gullible than Herbert would be questioning a lot of what she was saying. This was why she had chosen him. Well, that and the fact that he was the town's biggest gossip.

She shook her head gravely. "I wouldn't like to say, Herbert. You know, having a shop means I must adhere to strict rules and that there are constant checks that all food substances are handled correctly. I must admit to not being sure if the rules are as vigorous for some random girl on a rickety bicycle."

It niggled Juliana to refer to a grown woman as a girl, but she knew what would work with Herbert and, more importantly, what would work with all the people he chatted to all day long. She had to make them all mistrust Cherry, and this was the quickest way.

She accepted the flowers from Herbert and said goodbye, noting his preoccupation. It convinced her that rumours of Cherry's ice cream not being stored properly were about to start spreading through Wilmsford at any second.

She breathed in the scent of the lovely flowers, hoping this gesture hid what could no doubt be misconceived as a villainous smirk from anyone watching her.

She had promised her brother that she would win this war, and now she had dealt her enemy a crippling blow.

TEN

Reality Check

SOMETHING WAS MOST DEFINITELY UP. The people of Wilmsford, mainly middle-class mums and older people, were not subtle. So, when Cherry noticed more than one person whispering and then veering away from her, she knew something wrong.

Sales had been sliding for a couple of days. It wasn't anything dramatic at first, but by the first afternoon, she knew she wouldn't sell out that day. The second day had been even worse.

She tapped her fingers on the freezer box, watching as an elderly couple whispered to each other while looking in her direction.

What is going on? she wondered.

Initially, she had thought she'd stopped being the interesting new thing in town. Of course the novelty of an ice cream-selling trike would soon wear off and sales would start to slide, but she hadn't expected that to happen in a forty-eight hour period.

Out of the corner of her eye, she noticed a woman in her forties walking towards her. She didn't look like she was intending to enjoy an ice cream. She looked like she was about to enlist Cherry into some kind of political party. Or an army.

She was fearsome-looking, with not a trace of a smile on her face. She had a tight grip on a clipboard as she made a beeline towards Cherry.

"Good afternoon, fancy a free sample?" Cherry asked.

"No, I'd like you to answer some questions." The woman stood in front of Cherry and stared down at her. She was the sort of woman who got things done, the woman the town would go to in order to write a strongly worded letter or begin a petition. She was not the sort of woman to have a scoop of Chunky Monkey on a warm spring afternoon.

"Sure, fire away," Cherry said.

The woman pointed at the freezer between the two front wheels of the trike. "I'd like the specifications for *that.*"

Cherry frowned. "You're interested in buying one?"

"No. I'm ascertaining if it is fit for purpose." The woman sneered at the freezer as if it was personally responsible for all the wrongs in the world.

"Can I ask why you think it might not be fit for purpose?" Cherry asked. The woman's attitude was getting on her nerves, but she knew better than to let her stress show. The key to dealing with awkward people was to stay calm and collected. The answer to why her customers were staying away might be right in front of her, clutching a clipboard to her heaving chest and looking like she wanted to set fire to Cherry's parasol.

"I heard that a child got sick after eating here."

"What?!" Cherry couldn't stay calm at that insinuation. "Who? What happened?"

"That's what I'm trying to find out."

"Well, I can assure you that my ice cream is perfectly safe."

"I hear you make it at home, in your bathroom?"

Cherry rolled her eyes and stared up at the sky, willing whatever being might dwell there to give her strength.

"Really? In my bathroom?"

"That's what I heard."

"That's preposterous," Cherry replied.

"So, you're saying you don't make it in your bathroom?"

Cherry took a deep breath. "My ice cream is not homemade; it's made by a supplier who have all their food hygiene certificates in order. I provide them with flavour combinations, and they make them for me. I'll give you their details, but you'll see from the pack I submitted to the council that my supplier is complying with every food safety regulation there is."

Cherry gestured for the woman to follow her to the side of the freezer and pointed to a label on the bottom.

"This bad boy is a Mobiluxo 12-volt freezer. I plug it in when I get home, and it recharges overnight. It stays cool at up to minus twenty-five degrees for up to twelve hours. I trade for eight hours, give or take, and it takes me an hour to travel to and from my house to here. Do you hear that noise?"

The woman put her head against the side of the freezer and nodded.

"That's the battery working. It's keeping the ice cream frozen. At no point does that freezer ever turn off." Cherry stood up and tapped a display. "You can see here what the temperature is inside the freezer."

Cherry opened the lid, making some of the cold air escape as vapour. "As you can see, it's glacially cold in here." She picked up the thermometer from inside the freezer and handed the icy metal device to the woman.

"This is my back-up, in case the display is wrong. Now, ice cream is actually supposed to be stored at temperatures colder than your average frozen food." She snatched the thermometer out of the woman's hand and threw it back into the freezer, slamming the lid closed. "So, where most frozen food should be stored between minus twelve and minus eighteen, the Food Standards Agency recommends more like minus-twenty, which my freezer can handle no problem at all. It might be a problem if I overload it, but I never do. In fact, I spend half an hour every morning checking what I have stored, weighing the ice cream, and ensuring it's packed correctly."

Cherry opened the storage box on the back of her trike and pulled out all her paperwork. She handed it to the woman. "There. That's all my certificates, supplier's information, permit, storage plans, stock levels. Everything. As you can see, there is nothing wrong with my ice cream."

The woman looked stunned. She stared down at the paperwork which Cherry had dumped in her hands.

"Morning, Mary." Another officious-looking woman walked by. "Did you hear? The Lawson boy didn't have food poisoning. He swallowed a Lego figurine."

Clipboard Woman, Mary, turned to stare at the passer-by. "What?"

"I think it was Iron Man," the other woman shouted over her shoulder as she walked away.

Mary slowly turned back towards Cherry, ashen faced.

Cherry folded her arms and glared. "Am I to assume that the Iron Man gobbler was the boy you thought I poisoned?"

Mary let out a nervous laugh. "Well, you know what it's like! Rumours get out of hand in a small town like this."

"Rumours like this could bankrupt me," Cherry replied.

Mary looked contrite. "I really am sorry. You just hear so many stories of rogue traders, I wanted to make sure that you were operating above board."

"Have I convinced you?" Cherry asked.

"Absolutely." Mary nodded and handed back all the paperwork. "I can see you know what you are talking about, and your freezer clearly works exceptionally well. You obviously have all your certificates in place. I am sorry, really."

Cherry breathed out a sigh of relief. As hurtful as it was to be accused of something as terrible as poor food preparation and storage, at least she now knew why people had been avoiding her.

"Mary, is it?" she asked.

The woman nodded.

"Mary, I don't mind telling you that I'm very upset by all of this," she confessed. "Would you consider helping me out and trying to put these rumours to rest? All I'm trying to do is make a living and spread a little sunshine with some fun ice cream."

Mary nodded so quickly that she might have pulled a muscle. "Of course, absolutely! I'll spread the word that I've seen all your certificates and spoken to you. I'll reassure everyone that there's nothing to worry about."

"That would be very much appreciated." Cherry breathed a sigh of relief. "The proof's in the eating. Can I offer you a free sample now?"

Mary smiled. "Oh, go on then, just a little one."

Cherry prepared an ice cream for Mary, a little

one turning into quite a big one with sprinkles. Mary placed her clipboard on top of the freezer unit to fully focus on the ice cream. She gushed about how delicious it was while telling Cherry about her position as a volunteer at the council, the school, the church, the trader's association, and more.

Cherry listened, feeling like a bartender who nodded along to customers' tales. Mary wasn't a bad person; she was just passionate. She loved Wilmsford and wanted to make sure it was as safe and secure as possible. She could probably do with staying in her lane a little more, but Cherry wasn't about to say so.

Mary was already promising to get the rumours quashed and explained that her influence was so wide-ranging that she imagined Cherry would have a long queue by the next morning.

Cherry hoped she was right. Her fall from grace had been a shock, and while she hoped that it was now sorted, she couldn't help but wonder how it had all started. Small towns were full of rumours, but they all started somewhere. This one had started rather quickly.

She glanced over at the Gelato Parlour.

She wouldn't, Cherry mused. *Would she?*

"Mary, can I ask where you first heard this rumour?" Cherry interrupted the woman's rambling about her new basset hound.

"Oh, I think it was Diane. Who heard from Julie. I

think she overheard it from Pat and Margie. And they probably heard it from Herbert."

Cherry turned around and looked down the street at Old Herbert, the florist. In her experience, it was true that most gossip came from him. She'd even seen him running up the street once to share a particularly juicy piece of gossip with a group of older women.

Suddenly, Cherry recalled Juliana walked up the high street a couple of evenings ago. She'd been clutching a bouquet of flowers and looking mightily pleased with herself. It had caught Cherry's eye because she'd wondered if Juliana had received the flowers as a gift, if the woman was dating. Then she quickly shook her head and reminded herself that she didn't care about such things.

It was all coming together. Juliana had spread some kind of rumour to Herbert, and the very next day, Cherry's business took a nosedive.

She narrowed her eyes and stared at the Gelato Parlour.

Two could play at that game.

ELEVEN

Living off Espressos and the Blood of Puppies

JULIANA STOOD by the Gelato Parlour's window, crossed her arms over her chest, and shook her head at the long queue to Cherry's blasted bicycle. Deep down, she was once again impressed by the resilience and dogged determination of this woman. How had Cherry managed to stop the rumours so easily? How did she pull off these swift miracles?

She squinted so she could watch Cherry assemble a cone with a scoop of something powder blue and another of something neon pink. What kind of food was that colour? Still, the child who received it was thrilled, and Cherry's responding smile lit up the entire street.

Something in Juliana niggled and itched. It had to be curiosity. She convinced herself that she needed to see what the competition was doing, to see what disgusting concoctions Cherry was selling and what she told people to make them buy from her despite rumours of bad food practices flying around. There was a reluctance, which felt almost like apprehension, buried in her stomach. She ignored it and let the rest of her body radiate nonchalance as she strode out toward her competition.

Juliana was thinking of something clever and condescending to say to get Cherry's attention when she noticed something. Cherry On Top's ridiculous homemade menu had a new flavour: "Snobbish and Dull Lemon Sorbet".

Juliana sucked in a breath. Lemon sorbet was her biggest seller. And "dull" was Cherry's favourite word to describe the Gelato Parlour. There was no doubt what Cherry was doing here.

That petty, devious bimbo!

Right at that moment, Cherry had finished serving a customer and peered over at Juliana.

"Well now, if it isn't Wilmsford's own ice queen. What are you doing here? You must be scouting for business pointers because I know you didn't come here for the ice cream. Everyone knows you live off espressos and the blood of puppies."

"Excuse me?" Juliana snarled.

"Well, look at you," Cherry said, eyeing Juliana's body. "Skinny as a rake and bitter as coffee grounds." She turned to her customers. "There's no way this woman eats ice cream, is there, kids? She doesn't like nice food. Or being nice."

The children all giggled, and Juliana saw a few parents barely hiding smirks.

Juliana arranged her face to not show her fury. "Oh, and you're always nice, dear? Is that what you're saying? Is your new flavour a sign of that?" she said, stabbing a finger onto the hurtfully named lemon sorbet. "Furthermore, do you still claim that we're not competing, hm? While you're selling *sorbets*?"

"Would you mind asking one damn question at a time?" Cherry replied with a launch forward that nearly upset the trike. She was angrier than Juliana had seen her since the bin incident. "Sorry about the language," Cherry added to her customers, adjusting a few strands of hair which had gone flying during her outburst.

She really did convey all her emotions with her body language.

Juliana made a mental note that Cherry didn't do well when asked many questions at a time. That could be a useful weapon for her next attack.

She hid her own rage so that she could have the upper hand. Then she tilted her head, forcing out the patronising smile that she knew infuriated people. "You know what, Ms Hawkins? I don't think there is much point in me asking you questions. I know all your answers. You are intensely predictable, as you have about as much depth as an evaporated puddle."

"Oh bugg… I mean, go away!" Cherry bellowed.

"Gladly," Juliana roared back.

She spun around and marched back into the Gelato Parlour and then into her office. She slammed the door shut and leaned against it, breathing hard. She was overheating and wafted her shirt as much as she could, considering how figure-hugging it was. This was ridiculous. She was a Martin-Sinclair. Her family were known for having control over everything, including their own emotions. Juliana shouldn't let anyone take her control from her. She shouldn't let anyone take *anything* from her.

"Snobbish and dull lemon sorbet," she whispered to herself.

How dare that woman-child goad her like this? How dare she stock Juliana's biggest seller *and* mock it at the same time? Wasn't it enough that Cherry was threatening her livelihood? How did she even know to target the sorbet? Had she been asking around? Had she been talking to Aaron? Who could Juliana trust now?

She regarded her trembling hands. She felt like she could see the control slipping through her fingers and down to the cold, hard floor. Her heart was racing. Why did she let this woman do this to her? Why couldn't she get rid of her? Cherry Hawkins was like an unstoppable force, ploughing forward without mercy and making everyone love her as she did.

Juliana gave a hollow chuckle. Fate was playing a cruel joke, making her admire Cherry even while she hated her.

Maybe she should call Eduardo? Or her parents? They might have some ideas. No. She was a thirty-seven-year-old woman and had to fight her own battles. She had to trust herself.

She took a long inhale through her nose and let it out through her mouth.

Then she did it again.

And again.

Her heartbeat was calming down now. Control was seeping back in with the fresh oxygen filling her lungs. Juliana straightened until she stood ramrod straight with her chin up, chest out, and her jaw set. She could handle Cherry. She would devise a plan, even if that plan had to be bolder and crueller than anything she'd tried before.

I'll get rid of the ginger bimbo if it's the last thing I do!

TWELVE

Murder on the Pedestrianised Area

IT WAS the end of the day, and Cherry had almost sold out of stock. It had been a couple of days since she'd recruited Mary's assistance in quashing the rumours about any food safety issues, and business was booming again.

She was furious that Juliana had struck such a low blow. Not that she had actual evidence that she was the culprit, just a very, very strong suspicion.

Cherry couldn't imagine doing something so dastardly. She'd tossed and turned all night wondering what she would do to retaliate. Nothing seemed appropriate. Cherry wasn't one for underhanded games. She resolved any issues she might have through dialogue, like a grown-up. Juliana may have been older than she was, but she most certainly wasn't more mature.

Eventually, Cherry had decided to hit Juliana where

it hurt. In the freezer. More specifically, the sorbet section.

If Juliana was going to be all snobby about selling sorbets and gelato, then Cherry would happily make room for one of Juliana's most boring flavours.

The single sorbet sold well, not as well as the ice creams, but people were willing to try it despite her cheeky signage. She'd hoped that word would get back to Juliana, but the stars aligned when the woman saw the sign herself.

Cherry wasn't proud of the shouting match that had followed, especially since it had happened in front of customers, but Juliana was impressively clever and really knew how to push her buttons.

The high street was emptying, and Cherry decided it was time to give up for the day. She pulled the parasol from its holder and closed it, slotting it back in place. She locked the freezer and paused. She bit her lip and lightly pressed below her stomach.

"Dammit," she mumbled. "World's smallest bladder strikes again."

She knew from experience to not attempt to cycle home when she needed the bathroom. Bike riding and full bladders didn't mix.

She checked that everything was secure before hurrying to the public toilets around the corner. She passed a couple of shopkeepers having a conversation as they lowered the shutters to their neighbouring shops. They were laughing and joking, seeming like they had been friends forever.

Cherry sighed. She wished she could have that kind of relationship with Juliana. The last thing she wanted was to be in the middle of some turf war. It wasn't in her nature to fight with people. Her mum had always encouraged her to kind, helpful, and respectful, but she'd also told her to stand up for herself.

Stocking a sorbet flavour had obviously upset Juliana. Cherry felt a little guilty afterwards, until she reminded herself that Juliana had attempted to spread terrible rumours about her business.

Still, she had to wonder if this tit-for-tat behaviour was helping anyone. She didn't like fighting, even if it was against someone as rude as Juliana. If she could push a button and magically fix everything between them, she would.

As Cherry washed and dried her hands, she realised that she hadn't tried her hardest to placate Juliana. Maybe if they sat down over a coffee, they would realise they had more in common than they thought. Maybe they could come to some kind of an agreement.

She blew out a breath. She didn't really *want* to approach Juliana. She had started the battle, so why should she make efforts to end it?

She shook her head. It was something to consider another day, one where she wasn't exhausted from hours standing out in the sun. What she needed now was to cycle home, plug in the trike, collapse on the sofa, and enjoy a well-earned rest.

On the way back to her pitch, she could hear the distant sounds of shops closing up: the rattling of shutters, alarm panels beeping their codes, vehicles driving away. Above everything she could hear an engine and the loud, steady beeps of a vehicle reversing.

She rounded the corner and stopped dead in her tracks. An enormous lorry was reversing down the pedestrian path, *Pete's Sofas* emblazoned on its side. Right behind the behemoth truck was her beloved trike.

"WAIT!" Cherry screamed.

The warning beeps drowned out her cry.

"STOP!" she tried again, dashing towards the lorry and her livelihood.

There was nothing she could do. Her trike was caught up under the giant, eighteen-wheel truck. She skidded to a halt and stared at the mangled remains as it passed under all three rear wheels.

The lorry paused its movement.

"What was that?" Cherry heard a male voice ask.

"Nothing, you're fine, keep backing up."

Cherry felt her blood run cold at the sound of Juliana's voice from the other side of the lorry.

The lorry continued. Cherry stood there, helpless. She watched as another set of wheels went over her beloved trike. Pieces of it were still cracking and bending under the weight of the lorry and Pete's new delivery.

Finally, the cab and the final set of wheels cleared.

Cherry stared at the ground. The fate of her business was clear to see. The trike was flattened. The wheels were crushed, the freezer in pieces, her parasol torn to shreds. There was nothing left.

She slowly lifted her head and looked at the woman standing opposite her. Juliana looked apologetic, or some version of it. If someone could look gleeful and sorry at the same time, they'd look just like Juliana in that moment.

"I'm sorry, I didn't see it there," she said, her voice breaking a little. "I was just helping Pete to reverse up, so he didn't hit the tree. I thought you'd left for the day."

Cherry didn't know if she believed her or not. Sadness and fury warred within her, and she didn't know which one would win. She didn't know if she would pick up the tattered remains of her parasol and weep into the fabric or if she would pick up what remained of her handlebars and beat Juliana to death with them.

"I…" She trailed off, having no idea what to say.

Pete got out of the cab of the truck and stood by the shattered remains of the trike. He scratched his head.

"Who put that there?" he asked.

THIRTEEN

Flamingo-Pink with Eyelashes

JULIANA SWALLOWED A HOT MOUTHFUL, barely tasting the dark chocolaty bitterness left on her tongue. She was on her second espresso and her ninth Cherry-free day. The latter made her squirm in her office chair. She had been so sure that the best way to handle the competition would be to eliminate the bicycle. Or rather, the trike. That was what the vehicle was actually called, she'd finally come to admit, when Cherry had, ashen faced and shivering with shock, told Juliana that she'd murdered her trike.

Juliana scoffed to herself. *Murder. What an exaggeration.*

What did Cherry expect after her underhanded bribing and buttering up of the council? The only way out that she'd left Juliana was playing dirty.

Still, she had to admit that it had hurt to see Cherry's beautiful face so twisted with anguish when Pete ran over the trike. The fury that followed had actually been an improvement. Juliana had planned to only let Pete accidentally damage the trike a little, enough to make Cherry see that Juliana Martin-Sinclair was not to be trifled with, that she should move her business elsewhere. Except, when Pete was reversing that giant lorry of his, there was no small denting or slight damaging. It was all or nothing. So, she'd let him flatten the trike. No, if she was being honest, she'd *made* him crush it.

Juliana straightened. She hadn't done anything she wouldn't do again. The guilt she felt was unavoidable, but satisfaction and relief overshadowed it. The Gelato Parlour was safe. Her customers had returned and were now buying more than just hot drinks. In fact, when she'd last checked on the shop, she'd spotted a local celebrity, the wife of a famous football player, buying double mocha gelatos and vanilla lattes for her whole gaggle of friends.

Juliana finished her espresso while absentmindedly smoothing her hair. It wasn't as neat as she liked. She'd have to let it down so she could comb it through before returning it to its ponytail. While doing so, she sighed at her reflection in the office's mirror. This dispute with Cherry, leading to the loss of control and financial worry, had made her lips pallid and her black hair sprout a couple of grey strands. There were dark circles under her eyes, too. She recognised the signs of sleeplessness and stress. She wondered if Cherry, wherever she was these days, had been suffering from stress as well.

She applied some lipstick before starting to brush her tresses with excessive force. She stopped mid-stroke when she heard Aaron call her name. Something in his voice made her put the brush down right away. She hurried out into the shop and saw him staring out the window with his mouth agape. She followed his gaze and saw one of the most dreadful things she'd ever forced her poor eyeballs to take in.

Driving at a snail's pace up the pedestrian area was a flamingo-pink, ancient Citroën van. It had those hideous eyelashes glued onto its headlights and a sign on its side reading: *Cherry on Top*.

Right as Juliana was about to start inwardly cursing the ginger bimbo, she saw the woman herself. She was smiling in the driver's seat and staring right through the window into Juliana's eyes as she coasted along at her leisure. To make the nightmare worse, Cherry gave a slow, theatrical wink and then pushed the horn, which played a long, awful ditty.

"Huh," Aaron said from Juliana's side. "I've never heard a car horn play the theme from *The Muppets* before."

It was a good thing Cherry was still honking that horn. The chipper melody drowned out some of the filthy curse words escaping Juliana's lips.

FOURTEEN

Back in Business

CHERRY COULDN'T SEE Juliana very well through the tinted window, but she could see enough to tell that the woman was rigid, presumably with rage. And rightly so, Cherry had spent ages picking a vehicle that was hideous enough to push all of Juliana's buttons.

At first, she'd considered a standard ice cream van, one with a plastic ice cream cone mounted to the roof that acted as a speaker, playing "Pop! Goes The Weasel" at random intervals. It had been tempting to purchase, especially considering the weasel bit.

Then she'd laid her eyes on her new love. Harry. She'd called it Harry because it was a Citroën H Van. The owner hadn't been able to tell her what the H stood for, so Cherry had dutifully obliged by naming her new vehicle.

It was cheap, probably because it had been built in the fifties, but that just gave Cherry more money for improvements, like the hot-pink paint job, the speciality horn, and the eyelashes on the front.

The engine was… interesting. It spluttered and coughed when going up even the slightest hill and made an interesting whirring noise when idling, but, as far as Cherry was concerned, that was a small matter. The actual van was perfection.

She had a seat, a proper, padded leather one, and she no longer had to pedal. Not to mention the fact that she had space, bags of it. She could walk around the inside of the van, opening up both sides to customers with a hatch and a drop-down shelf.

She was no longer confined to one freezer; she now had four. She didn't have enough ice cream to put in them all, but she'd figure that out later. The possibilities were endless.

A-board sign, fairy lights, and her Cherry on Top signage completed the look. No one in Wilmsford would be able to miss her now.

She pulled up, ensuring that the rear of Harry was pointed in the direction of the Gelato Parlour. Perhaps it was childish, but she found it enormously satisfying to present Juliana with the arse end of her van. She figured she'd alternate: arse one day, headlight eyelashes the next.

Feeling around for the door handle, she yanked open the stiff lever and the suicide door swung loose. It would take a little while to get used to backwards doors. She hopped out and took in a breath of fresh air. It was good to be back.

She counted to five in her head, plastered a big smile on her face, and headed straight into the Gelato Parlour. Aaron was serving a customer, one of the few who didn't have their eyes clued to the window, looking at Harry with fascination.

Juliana stood behind the counter, her cheeks flushed. Cherry didn't know if she was angry or frightened.

"I just came in to say thank you," Cherry said. She leaned on the glass of the sorbet cabinet and smiled warmly at Juliana.

"Thank you?" The woman looked mightily confused.

"Yes. If you hadn't accidentally crushed my beloved trike, then I wouldn't have been in the market for a better vehicle. The insurance payout was good, and I had the profits from the few weeks when I was trading, so I bought Harry."

"Harry?"

"Yup. Isn't he a beauty?"

Juliana slowly turned her head to look out of the window. "It's pink."

"He is. Hot pink. Special order colour."

"And you called it Harry?"

"Yes, he likes pink. Don't judge." Cherry gazed adoringly at Harry. "He's great. So, thank you. Now I have a new, brighter, louder, sturdier vehicle. And an extra wheel! I'm four-wheel people now."

"So I see." Juliana didn't look at all pleased. In fact, Cherry was pretty sure she was attempting to cover up a wince.

"I can store so much more ice cream," Cherry continued. "Who knows? I might branch out into gelato!"

Juliana's striking dark eyes narrowed.

"Or coffee. I have a power supplier now. Isn't it exciting to think of all the possibilities?" She returned Juliana's glare.

"Cool van," Aaron said, clearly unaware that the two women were in the middle of a death-stare competition.

"Thanks, Aaron," she said cheerfully. "My mummy helped me paint him. And I know she'd be very, very upset if anything happened to him."

"Him?" Aaron asked.

"Harry," Cherry repeated.

"Oh. Cool name."

"Thank you."

"It can't be legal," Juliana said, waking up from her trance.

"It's got an MOT," Cherry argued. "It passed inspection."

Juliana placed her hands on either side of her slim waist. "I mean, for your permit. They are very specific. That thing is very different to a bike."

"Trike," Cherry corrected.

"Quite."

"Well, I checked, and it says I can park a non-permanent vehicle there. Harry is non-permanent. So, you'll be seeing him every… single… day." She stared at Juliana for a few more seconds before standing up and smiling. "Better go set up. Toodles!"

As Cherry walked out of the Gelato Parlour, a few people complimented her on Harry and commiserated about the frightful demise of her trike. She offered them all a free ice cream, enjoying the interesting shade of red Juliana was going as she did so.

FIFTEEN

The Ginger Nut Has Upgraded to Four Wheels

IT TOOK ABOUT five seconds of slow blinking and rapid breathing for Juliana to decide what to do. During those five seconds she had time to consider the following: screaming, kicking the wall, and kidnapping Cherry to strand her on the moon. She chose a more level-headed plan: calling Colin the Toad to see if anything could be done.

She rushed to the Gelato Parlour's office and rifled through her handbag for her phone. She found his number in her contacts and stabbed the call icon on the screen. It rang for far too long.

"Colin Greene speaking," he answered in a lazy tone of voice.

"Oh, so you finally bothered to pick up? This is Juliana Martin-Sinclair. I need to speak to you about Cherry Hawkins."

There was a sound on the other end which could

have been a muffled groan. "Juliana, we've already talked about the lovely Cherry and her right to sell her wares in that particular spot."

She ground her teeth before replying. "Yes. I know. This is a different conversation."

He sighed. "Very well. What is it now?"

"The ginger nut has upgraded to four wheels."

There was a beat of silence on the call.

"I… what… Are you feeling okay? I mean, was that even English?" Colin asked, sounding about as intelligent as a drowsy amoeba.

"Cherry returned this morning, after the unfortunate accident with her vehicle, and is now selling her ice cream from a large van. A van! Surely that goes against her permit regulations?"

"Hold on a moment," Colin said.

Juliana could hear him whispering with someone in the background, probably his secretary or whomever else they put in charge of handling this useless windbag. Seconds ticked by, and Juliana's rage grew.

"I have now consulted her permit," Colin suddenly said.

No, you consulted with someone who checked it for you, she thought. All she said out loud was, "And?"

"As long as it is sanitary, doesn't hinder foot traffic, and is non-permanent—meaning that she can remove it by end of trading hours each day—Cherry Hawkins can sell her products out of any sort of vehicle."

Juliana balled her free hand into such a tight fist

that her knuckles whitened and her nails dug into her palm. It was as Cherry had said, then. It pained Juliana to admit it, but her competition was smart—surprising, considering her bumbling behaviour, exasperating exuberance, and general lack of taste.

She put all her control into making her voice sound reasonable and professional. "I see. Well, I think that the van might be breaking other rules, such as how it stands out in our refined, picturesque town centre."

"You mean its appearance breaks Wilmsford's aesthetic statutes?" Colin asked.

"I mean that it is a huge, shabby, fluorescent eyesore that not only generates terrible noise and fumes, but also makes our pedestrianised area resemble cheap carnival grounds!"

"Oh. Hm. While I'm sure it's not that bad, it does sound like I should come inspect it. Hold a moment, please."

There was more whispering as he obviously asked his assigned grown-up what his schedule was and if he was allowed to leave the office. "It looks like I can pop into town at about three p.m., although I can't stay for long."

Juliana's tight chest loosened a tiny bit. "That's fine. I'm sure a quick glance will convince you of how inappropriate this vehicle is."

"Mm. Well, we'll see. If nothing else, it will give me a chance to get another free ice cream from our delightful Cherry. So yummy!"

He was actually rubbing the ice cream bribery in her face, admitting it freely. When it came to the "yummy" comment, Juliana wasn't sure if he meant the ice cream or Cherry, but judging from the tone of voice, it was likely the latter. It made her skin crawl. She got the feeling that the toad was trying to make her feel jealous or threatened. But jealous of what? Threatened by what? That he preferred Cherry's ice cream over her sorbets and gelatos? Or that he preferred Cherry over her?

Or that Cherry prefers him over you?

This last thought confused her, and she quickly pretended it had never entered her mind. She forced her clenched fist to relax before her fingernails, despite their shortness, drew blood.

"Are you still there?" Colin asked. "Let me guess, you're seething over this ice cream affair, aren't you? You really must learn to relax. You're an attractive woman, if one likes your sort of look, but frown lines won't do you any favours," he said in a singsong. "You should smile more, like Cherry does."

Juliana's rage was now big enough and sabre-toothed enough that she couldn't subdue it for much longer. She had to hang up or she'd say something she regretted.

"I have to go, Colin. I'll see you this afternoon."

"Oh, what's that? Rushing off without even a thank you? You're as frantic and rude as your crabby father was when I had to work for him," Colin said. He hummed pensively. "You know, I'm surprised you haven't had a heart attack or something along those lines by now. All that coffee, no love life, so much anger, and now this unhealthy obsession with a pretty twenty-five-year-old."

Afraid of what she might say, Juliana hung up. She marched out to Aaron and asked, "Can you manage on your own for an hour or two?"

He scratched his beard in bewilderment. "Yeah, sure. Everything all right?"

"No," she barked. Seeing the look on his face, she softened her tone to add, "It will be after three o'clock this afternoon, though. Right now, I'm going home to change and go for a run. I need to clear my head and vent some anger."

"Okay, sounds like a good idea, boss. Don't worry, I'll man the fort."

"Thank you. I'll be back as soon as I can," Juliana said as she turned to leave.

"Man, that pavement is going to get the crap pounded out of it," she heard him mumble to himself as she left.

SIXTEEN

Unwanted Help

IF CHERRY HAD KNOWN that selling ice cream from a hot-pink, eyelash-adorned, seventy-year-old van would be such a hit, she would have tried it earlier.

People *loved* Harry. In fact, they loved him so much that Cherry was already thinking about a range of merchandise dedicated to the van. She was sure that the locals would love T-shirts and hoodies featuring Harry's unique look.

She'd only been trading for a few hours and had already completely sold out of her top flavour. If she'd had a run of customers like this when she'd had the trike, she'd be cycling home already, sold out for the day.

Thankfully, Harry allowed her to hold more stock, which meant she could trade for longer, sell more, and make more profit. This was good because, as much as she adored her new van, she was pretty sure it needed a major refit.

She'd obtained a food safety certificate with ease, but there was rust around the main body of the van that sometimes let shafts of light in. Cherry wasn't a mechanic, but even she knew that wasn't good news. There was a spot on the floor that groaned like an eighty-year-old getting out of bed whenever she stepped on it. Harry was the new love of her life, but even so, he was an old man who desperately needed some replacement hips.

Maybe when it breaks down, I'll get Juliana to set fire to it so I can claim on the insurance for this vehicle, too, she wondered.

This thought reminded her that she was still livid with Juliana. The coffee-swilling monster had deliberately flattened her beloved trike. She chewed the inside of her cheek thoughtfully.

It was hard to be angry with someone who had triggered the series of events that led to her buying Harry. She had a stool she could sit on when she wasn't serving customers; she had shelter from the hot rays of sun or the occasional shower. Harry was better than her trike in every single way.

"Damn her," Cherry mumbled, even so.

"Knock knock!" Someone rapped their knuckles on the side of the van, and Cherry was sure she saw a rivet fall from the ceiling.

Colin Greene's smug face appeared at the open

serving hatch. He leaned on the shelf and took in the insides of the van. "Well, well, look who's moving up in the world! Very nice."

Cherry forced a smile onto her face. "Thank you, Mr Greene."

"Colin, please," he reminded her.

He could say it again and again, but Cherry enjoyed the distance the formality wedged between them.

"I've been asked to come out and check that your new vehicle is in keeping with the terms of your permit," he explained.

"Oh, I wonder who asked you to do that." She rolled her eyes, although she had to admit to being amused by Juliana's predictability. "I did call your department. They told me that it was fine. It's a non-permanent vehicle, and there is nothing in the town charter about the colour scheme. I checked that, too."

"Good girl," Colin said. "I knew you'd be on top of everything. You are Cherry on Top after all."

Cherry chuckled along with him, not feeling the humour in the slightest.

"Where's the door?" he asked, looking around. He spotted the handle on the back door and grinned. "Ah, I see it. Let me come in and have a look."

Cherry felt her heart sink. The previously spacious interior was about to feel terribly cramped. She wanted to ask why Colin needed to come inside the van in order to check if it was suitable for her permit, but she also didn't want to upset the man who could revoke said permit in a heartbeat.

She blew out a breath, opened the back door to the van, and gestured for him to step up and inside. The floor had been lowered to allow people to stand upright in the back, but Colin's height meant he still had to crouch a little.

Cherry was secretly grateful that it would be uncomfortable for him as presumably that meant he'd leave all the sooner.

He looked around, opening and closing freezers and checking various bits of equipment. Cherry nervously shifted from foot to foot.

"I'm sorry about the trike," Colin said. "I heard it was an accident, but with Juliana and her temper, who knows?"

"Yeah, she kinda has it in for me."

"That she does. Did you turn her down for a date or something?" Colin laughed. He squirted some chocolate sauce onto his finger and licked it.

Cherry blinked. "Date?"

"Yeah, she's… you know. One of them. Lesbian." Colin whispered the last word, then suddenly looked sheepish. "Unless… you are as well? I mean, you don't look like one. But neither does she, I guess."

What does he think a Sapphic woman looks like? Are we all meant to look like carbon copies of Ellen DeGeneres?

"I'm bi," Cherry confessed, hoping it would stop Colin from saying anything else on the subject. She didn't know why, but the knowledge that Juliana was interested in women was causing a riot of emotions within her. "Anyway, I'm okay with the permit, right?"

Colin put down the chocolate sauce and sucked in a breath as he looked around the inside of the van. It was such a powerplay. He knew she was reliant on him, and he was soaking up the fact that he was the man in charge.

He slowly nodded. "Yep. I think we can square it all away. I'll deal with Juliana. She's a bitch, but I've had experience with her and her family, so I can put her in her place. Don't you worry."

Cherry couldn't stand being in the small space with him any longer. She stepped outside and started to fuss with one of the chalkboard signs that hung down from the serving hatch. "I appreciate that," she said, "but I can deal with Juliana. I just needed to know that my permit is valid and that the council are happy with the van. I mean, I've already had confirmation of that, but if you're saying it's fine as well?"

"You're all good," he confirmed.

Cherry let out a relieved sigh. The last thing she wanted was to have to suck up to him further. She just wanted to get on with selling ice cream. She would be fine battling Juliana by herself.

Colin stepped out the back of the van and continued his fake inspection. "As I say, Juliana is a bitch, but I'll keep you safe, Cherry."

Cherry kept her back to him and grimaced. She

couldn't imagine a thing he could do that would improve the situation. In fact, if Juliana felt about Colin the way Cherry did, he'd make things so much worse.

Not to mention the fact that she hated women being called *bitch*, especially by a man. Especially Juliana, even if she was perhaps the absolute dictionary definition of a bitch. Cherry sighed. She was tired and confused. She was starting to feel sorry for her number one tormentor.

"It's fine, really," she said. "I can deal with her. It's probably better if we keep it between Juliana and me anyway."

"Whatever you say," Colin replied. He leaned in close to her ear. "Just know that I'm on your side."

Cherry felt his hand lightly pat her bottom. She kept her back to him and gripped the chalk tight in her hand. She wanted to scream at him or smack him in the face, but she needed him, and she figured she could cope with a small brush of the hand, one that might have been accidental.

She hurried away from him, back to the safety of the van. "Thank you, Mr Greene."

He chuckled. "You'll call me Colin one day."

A customer appeared at the serving window, and Cherry quickly set about serving them, hoping that Colin would take the hint and leave. After a few minutes, she risked a glance up and was pleased to see that he had left.

The customer walked away, ecstatic with their

caramel crunch ice cream, and Cherry made a mental note to order some more. She looked at her watch and realised that it was time to pack up and head home.

All in all, her first day with Harry had been great, save for Colin's interruption at the end. She hoped that would be the end of it and that she wouldn't see the slimy man again for a while. She could take him in small doses, but the thought of another visit from him in the near future made her shiver.

SEVENTEEN

Do You Think I'm Shagging Her, Too?

JULIANA HAD SPRINTED around her usual running circuit until her lungs ached. Then she'd taken a shower so hot that her skin still tingled. That, and a nutritious lunch, led to a slightly calmer Juliana now standing by the window and awaiting Colin's inspection of Cherry's eyelashed, pink atrocity.

Juliana saw herself as too dignified to stare open-mouthed, but she gaped at the scene outside the window. She'd seen Colin arrive and Cherry give him that charismatic smile and toss those damned shiny, strawberry blonde tresses so they reflected the sunlight. Then she'd invited him into that cramped van with her. For an unreasonably long time, too. And when they finally came back out, there was that blatant caress of her backside. She'd let that toad of a man place his slimy, stubby-fingered hand on her bottom!

Cherry was a smart, hard-working, confident, and

attractive woman. Why would she let someone like *him* touch her? There was only one reason: to steal Juliana's customers and to prove that her new, modern products were better than hers. How dare Cherry put feminism back seventy years just to sell ice cream!

She didn't know what made her angriest: Cherry sleeping her way to the top, Cherry ruining her livelihood, her own inability to keep control of the situation, much less her own emotions, or that the pea-brained, bigoted Colin Greene had been allowed to lay his disgusting hands on someone so extraordinary.

Whatever the answer, Juliana had seen enough. She told Aaron to man the counter, despite it being her shift, and stormed out. By the time she was by the van, Cherry had just finished serving a customer.

Colin was nowhere to be seen. Lucky for him as Juliana's blood was boiling again.

She pointed to Cherry. "How could you?"

Cherry took a step back from the van's selling hatch. "Stop screaming. What are you on about?"

"Don't you think I saw you? I'm right over there, Cherry. I can see when you seduce a councillor. I can see it when you bribe him with ice cream, when you flirt with him, and when you let him grope you in public. I suppose you're having sex with him?"

"What?! Are you insane? I can't believe you would come over here shouting at me and accusing me of stuff like that. Get out of my sight before I," she looked around the van, "throw all these sprinkles at you."

"Sprinkles? SPRINKLES? Is that the best you can do? I bet you gave Colin the Toad more than bloody sprinkles!"

A look of spite came over Cherry's face. "Is that what you want to hear, Juliana? What exactly is it that your paranoid, self-absorbed, dirty mind wants to hear? That I just let him take me on top of the chocolatey flavours?" she said, pointing to the ice creams on the right side of the display case.

A quick, stray thought popped into Juliana's mind. *So, she divides her ice creams into specific sections, too.* She shook her head and refocused. "No, I want the damned truth. Do you meet up with him after work? Did you only get a permit for this spot because you sleep with him and he wanted a way to mess with me? Are you two conspiring together against me?"

"Conspiring? Against *you*? Bloody hell. Do you hear yourself, Juliana? Why is this all about you?"

"Don't change the topic! Answer the question for once."

"I will when you ask one damned question at a time and when you stop shouting."

Juliana's fury made her heart pound so hard that all of Wilmsford must have been able to hear it. Trying to keep from screaming, she looked heavenward and scoffed. "You know, I thought you straight women had finally stopped exploiting the fact that there's heterosexual men who think with their genitals and can be manipulated through sex."

"First of all, I'm not straight, and you need to stop making assumptions about people. Secondly, I didn't bloody sleep with him!" Cherry screamed with frustration. "He touched my arse and I wasn't sure if it was an accident or a grope, but from your reaction I guess it was the nastier option. Now I'm even more pissed off, both at him for that and at you for victim blaming."

"Don't you dare pin this on me," Juliana growled. "I'd never victim-blame. I told you, I saw you smile at him, laugh at his boring jokes, and give him free ice cream. I saw you invite him into your van and then him coming out and grinning while licking his fingers."

"Ew! He did that to get chocolate sauce off them, not to get *me* off them." Cherry ran a hand over her grimacing face. "Look, I need to be nice to him so that he doesn't mess with my permit. Or take your side whenever we have our next little battle. Okay?"

"No, not okay. There's being nice, and then there's using your charm and perfect body as bait or as bargaining chips."

Cherry threw out her hands in a gesture of frustration, knocking over a bottle of caramel sauce. "Some people, unlike you, are polite and friendly. They smile. They give gifts. I was raised that way. It doesn't mean I want to wrap my legs around every person I do that for. Did you see me smiling at the old lady I just served? Do you think I'm shagging her, too?"

Juliana's jaw hurt from how tightly she'd been clenching it. "Maybe. Can she offer you a spot outside someone else's business so you can park your eyesore there and ruin their life instead?"

Cherry slammed the caramel sauce back into its holder. "I have not ruined your life, you cow!"

"You have all but ruined my business, and to me there isn't much difference," Juliana said through gritted teeth.

"You know what? I don't have to put up with this. Unlike you and your failing shop, I'm not stuck here." Cherry started securing things and closing up. "I can just drive off," she concluded as she got out of the van and shouldered past Juliana.

"Oh, please do, dear. I have been waiting for you to leave since the first moment you set foot—sorry, wheel—in my town."

Cherry paused from locking up the van's hatch and widened her eyes at Juliana. "Hang on, *your* town? You don't own Wilmsford! You have no rights to the customers who want ice cream." She opened the driver's door, a rusty piece of metal that was all but hanging off the frame. "And you certainly have no right to tell me what to do or to come here accusing me of shit!"

She climbed into the driver's seat and started to struggle with the seat belt while furiously muttering, "I can't believe you. Colin Greene? Of all people? You really think I'm capable of… that I'd…"

The ancient seat belt wouldn't clip into place. Cherry screamed in frustration before tossing the buckle off her and reaching for the door instead. She tried slamming it shut three times before it finally closed.

"I don't know what other conclusions I'm to draw from your behaviour," Juliana shouted over the revving engine.

Cherry stared daggers at her before crunching the van into gear. The old engine complained before the vehicle lurched into action. It took a few surges back and forth before the pile of rust finally started moving. It wasn't going that fast, but it was certainly making a lot of noise about it. Did Cherry go through this procedure every time she drove, or was her anger making the antique contraption's issues worse?

Driving away, the van swerved left and then right. Sudden unease made Juliana's stomach turn.

Why is she veering like that? Is she still struggling with the seat belt? Eyes on the road and drive properly, woman!

She could only watch as Cherry careened down the pedestrianised street and towards the side road that fed into the high street.

Juliana walked after the van, her stomach ache worsening as she heard another vehicle above the din of Cherry's. Something big was coming from the side road, and Cherry wasn't slowing down. Juliana craned her head and saw a white lorry.

For the briefest—but feeling like the longest—of moments, everything went deathly quiet.

A heartbeat later the lorry struck the pink van and

shoved it along as if it weighed nothing. Juliana's panic, terror, and shock made her want to scream. Maybe she did. She wasn't quite sure of what she was doing and feeling until she saw Cherry's van bounce out of the way of the lorry, remaining upright and intact, and could breathe again. Her relief made her dizzy.

The sounds around her returned and she waited, expecting Cherry to storm out of the van yelling that she could've been killed, shouting about the damage to her garish paintwork and claiming that it was all Juliana's fault.

That didn't happen. In fact, *nothing* happened.

Juliana's relief left her as fast as it had come. Sure, the van was on all four wheels and in one piece, but the fragile rust bucket had still been rammed out of the way at quite the speed.

The driver door opened, the backwards design causing it to slam against the wall of the van. Cherry stumbled out but quickly fell to the ground.

Juliana ran over as fast as her heels could carry her and crouched next to the prone woman, gently brushing Cherry's hair off her face so she could check on her.

"Can you hear me? Are you all right?" she asked, hearing her trembling voice break on the last word. "Answer me, Cherry. Please."

EIGHTEEN

Poor Harry

THE RINGING in her ears was deafening. Cherry couldn't quite figure out what had happened. She'd been driving home and now she was… lying on the street? Juliana was leaning over her, worry all over her usually composed face.

Cherry lifted a shaky hand and touched the wetness she felt on the back of her head. Her stomach lurched at the sight. White goo with swirls of red stained the tips of her fingers.

"Oh… is, is that my brain?" Cherry held her finger up towards Juliana. "Am I dying?"

Juliana sniffed Cherry's finger. "No, that smells like vanilla ice cream with some sort of berry sauce."

Cherry signed with relief. "Oh yeah. I had a tub of strawberry swirl near its expiry date on the seat next to me. I was going to throw it out when I got home," she mumbled.

"Is everything okay?" a male voice asked.

Cherry couldn't see him, but flashes of a lorry entered her memory.

Juliana's expression turned from worry to anger. She spun around.

"You have done quite enough damage here. I have your number, Simon Jones! Expect to hear from the police and from my solicitor! Get out of my sight before I strangle you with my own two hands."

Cherry winced at the increased volume but found the corner of her mouth curling into a smile. Juliana was looking after her, and somehow that made her feel good. If she ignored her splitting headache and aching body, anyway.

She heard Simon hurry away. Juliana turned back to her and lifted her hand to smooth Cherry's hair down.

"Is anything broken?" Juliana asked.

"Everything," Cherry mumbled. That was how it felt at least.

Juliana looked her over. "Let's start with the most important thing. Any dizziness, split vision, nausea, or confusion?"

"No. I mean, I don't feel any more confused than normally."

"Good, you're probably not concussed then. Can you move your legs?"

Cherry twitched her feet, and then bent her knees. She nodded.

Juliana reached her warm, soft hands around Cherry's head—she was surprised to find them warm and soft—and probed the back of her neck. "Any pain here?"

"No," Cherry whispered.

She ran gentle fingers meticulously across Cherry's head, parting her hair. "I can't feel any bumps either."

She removed her hands, and Cherry felt bereft. The woman knelt over her and worried her lip. "You were thrown about and then you collapsed when you tried to stand up. I can't tell if you're injured or not. I think you should go to the hospital."

"No! No, I'm fine, I'm fine." Cherry tried to push herself up but failed, twice. "I'll be fine, just need a little time. A lie-down. I'll be all good."

"I'm not letting you lay on the cold ground forever," Juliana argued. She pulled her mobile out of her pocket. "I'm calling an ambulance."

"No. Please, no!" Cherry reached up and grasped Juliana's wrist.

Juliana paused and looked at her, seemingly not worried that strawberry swirl from Cherry's fingers now stained her sleeve.

"Cherry, you've just been in a car crash," she said, her voice impossibly soft.

"I hate doctors. Like, really hate them. And hospitals. And ambulances. Please, I'm okay," Cherry begged. "I think I'm winded and bruised, but I don't need to go to hospital."

Juliana watched her for a few moments as she

seemingly weighed her options. After a while, she sighed and put the phone away. "Fine, but I'm taking you home. And if I think you have any broken bones, or require medical treatment, I *will* take you to the hospital. No arguments."

Bossy Juliana was back, but paired with her earlier tenderness, Cherry didn't mind. In fact, she was relieved to have someone there with her. She might've been trying to convince Juliana that she was fine, but she was in real pain. She hoped it was nothing serious.

She turned her head and looked at Harry. The driver's door lay open, and melting strawberry swirl ice cream dripped down the seat.

"Juliana?"

"Yes?"

"Is Harry okay?"

A frown line appeared between Juliana's beautiful eyes. "Harry?"

"My van."

"Oh. I don't know. I'm more worried about if *you* are okay."

"Poor Harry."

Juliana gently took her chin and turned her head away from the van. "Never mind Harry, let's focus on making sure you are okay."

"But—"

"I promise you, I'll make sure Harry is just fine."

NINETEEN

Mrs Hawkins Sips Her Tea

JULIANA SAT IN A WARM, cosy kitchen painted in creams and browns. It smelled of some sort of freshly baked pastries, ones that Juliana was sure she wasn't going to get to taste. A clock ticked softly somewhere out of view.

Everything was so homey and sweet that Juliana, in her stark clothes and intense perfume, felt like an invading foreigner, a feeling that was compounded by the behaviour of the homeowner: Cherry's mother, Hattie Hawkins. Not only did Mrs Hawkins have an alliterated name like a superhero, she also seemed to have X-ray vision like one. At least, if one was to judge by how she bored her gaze into Juliana's and seemed to know what her guest was thinking. This led to awkward small talk and to Mrs Hawkins refilling Juliana's mug of strong tea without having to check to see if it was time for a top-up. Uncanny.

Juliana hadn't wanted tea. She had been very clear on that. She'd been given one anyway. And then a refill. And now a top-up. Apparently, tea could magically fix shock and pretty much any other ailment and must be imbibed at all costs.

Juliana stared into her chipped mug of bitter tea and thought, *I'd kill for an espresso and a scoop of elderflower sorbet right now. No, this day calls for hazelnut gelato. Two big scoops. Preferably drenched in spiced rum.*

"So," Mrs Hawkins said after a sip of her tea. "While my Cherry gets some rest upstairs and you and I finish our cuppa, why don't we talk about the accidents that seem to happen in your area, hmm?"

Juliana stiffened. "Accidents? You mean what happened with the lorry today?"

"Not only that. There was her trike getting smashed to ruddy pieces, too," Hattie said, her clever eyes narrowing. "Freak accident that. Strange how these things happen, hmm?"

Juliana's collar was suddenly too tight. Why had she buttoned her shirt all the way up? "Yes. Strange."

Hattie sipped her tea. "Mm. And there have been some mishaps as well, haven't there?"

Juliana picked up her mug, too, mainly to hide her face. "I'm not sure what you're referring to."

"For example, your bin breaking and being stranded right where my Cherry had to try to sell foodstuff. That was pretty strange, too, wouldn't you say?"

Another squinting stare. Another sip of tea, this one halfway to a slurp.

Juliana resisted the urge to loosen her collar. Why did she feel like she was twelve and had been called into the headmistress's office for starting fights?

"Y-yes."

"I'd say so. And now my sweet, precious daughter is curled up in her bed with bruises and heaven knows what else."

The eye contact intensified to the point where Juliana thought it was going to make her head implode. "Cherry has… had some bad luck." She hesitated for only a second. "I'm certain that is about to change."

"You are?" Hattie slowly put her mug down, never dropping the eye contact. "Do you think these awful things are about to stop happening to my little girl, hmm?"

"I am convinced of it, Mrs Hawkins."

"Well, now, isn't that good news! I'm sure Cherry will be chuffed to hear it. Especially as she admires you."

Juliana choked while swallowing a mouthful of tea. "She *admires* me?"

"I'd say so. Even when she was complaining about you being mean to her, she always mentioned how stylish you looked, how formidable you were, how posh you spoke. Not to mention how you had your own shop selling ice creams."

"Gelatos and sorbets," Juliana corrected automatically. Hattie gave her a glare which made her add, "Not that the distinction is important."

"No, it's not. Anyway, I'm glad to hear that Cherry's bad luck is about to change." She smacked Juliana's upper arm with such force that she reeled. "See? I told you that if we had some tea, we could put the world to rights, Mrs Martin-Sinclair."

"It's miss, actually. But you can call me Juliana."

"Unmarried, then? I'll make sure to let Cherry know that."

"What?"

"Oh nothing, love," Hattie said, taking another sip from the mug that read, "World's Greatest Mum". This sip seemed more cheerful.

The drinking of beverages can't be cheerful. Get a grip, Juliana berated herself.

She was still rattled. That was all. If Cherry had been really injured, it would have been partly her fault. Maybe more than partly.

When she'd driven Cherry home, she'd tried to distract the younger woman from her pain and shock by pushing her to talk. That was when her passenger had explained—between whinging that she was dying and needed to draw up a will, but certainly not see a doctor—what had happened when Colin inspected the van. When they got stuck in traffic, Cherry had broken out in a barely coherent recap of the war between them from her point of view, only occasionally interrupted by the need for more reassurance that it really was strawberry swirl ice cream in her hair and not brain matter mixed with blood.

It was becoming clear to Juliana that Cherry was as whingey as a child when injured. On a more serious note, she was also realising that she'd misjudged Cherry's intentions. She really wasn't trying to cause trouble or win some sort of battle. She only wanted to sell ice cream. It seemed there wasn't a conniving or evil bone in that bruised body of hers. Cherry truly believed, naïve as it was, that they sold different products and therefore wouldn't be in competition. She had kept repeating, "I did some crappy things, but that was just when you pissed me off and I wanted a tiny bit of revenge," in a self-pitying voice.

Now there was a niggling worry in Juliana over what it meant that her first instinct was always that people were out to hurt her, mess with her, or take away her precious control and independence. She had to think about that. Unpleasant as it might be.

A clock chimed somewhere in the small but cosy terraced house. Juliana hadn't known that Cherry lived with her mother, nor that she lived in the outskirts of Wilmsford. For some reason, Juliana had thought of Cherry living somewhere farther away. Like some sort of cotton-candy dreamland. Or hell.

"It's nice that your daughter still lives with you," Juliana said with a smile she hoped looked genuine. "I know my mother still grieves the fact that my brother and I left home about fifteen years ago."

"Yes, I'm lucky to have her around. After her dad died, it was just the two of us."

The aching guilt that had taken root in Juliana's chest now spread its icy tendrils throughout her body. She forced herself to breathe. "Oh, I didn't know she lost her father. My condolences."

"Thank you. It was years ago, right as Cherry was finishing her high school and trying to decide what to do with her life. Not that she had to think much." Hattie gazed out the window with a nostalgic smile. "She's loved ice cream since she was a nipper and always wanted to work with it. It was just a matter of how and where. It's hard to set up a business without any contacts or much money. I'm afraid what little I could give her, her own savings, and her father's inheritance, all goes towards her student loan repayments. Oh, and it paid for that trike."

Juliana wanted to sink through the floor as the image of the flattened vehicle came to her mind.

Hattie snorted. "Oh, don't look so glum about the death of the trike. Cherry was happy in the end, since it paid for her Harry. Did you know that I painted that van?"

Since Juliana had nothing nice to say about Harry's paint job, she changed the topic. "You're right when you say it's hard to set up a new business. Especially on your own. Using my family name, I was lucky enough to have the contacts, but the money was another matter."

"Really?"

Sudden embarrassment heated Juliana's cheeks. Why had she brought that up? "Well, yes. My parents declined to lend me the money to start up my gelateria, so I had to save up for myself and scrape by until I could make a profit."

"You parents could've helped you but didn't? That's strange."

Juliana shrugged. "They wanted me to learn to be independent and take control of my own life. Also, they made it clear that they would have preferred it if I got a job in finance or at least started a business that was more prestigious than selling desserts and coffees."

"What's wrong with selling food?"

"Nothing if you ask me. My parents, however, felt it was frivolous. They have accepted my choice now, though." She paused before adding, "More or less."

Hattie picked up her mug again. "I'm sad to hear you didn't get any help, but at least that means you know how much blood, sweat, and tears it takes to start a business."

Juliana thought back to how her father's contacts on the council had helped her procure her store. It was in a great location but utterly rundown, which was the only reason she could afford it. She'd spent every waking moment trying to refurbish that place, first with the help of the least awful contractors in her price range and then on her own. After that, every remaining penny had gone to new plumbing, buying appliances, and decorating. The first few months, before the money started coming in, she'd been forced to sleep on Eduardo's sofa. Going home to her parents hadn't been an option. Nor had been asking them for help. They would never have let her live that down. She had to be in control of her own life. She had to be able to manage on her own.

Juliana swallowed hard, feeling like something jagged was stuck in the base of her throat. It would seem her parents and her upbringing were the source of her behavioural issues, maybe even the main reason any threat to the Gelato Parlour turned her into a ruthless wolf. After all, she had been ready to gobble up poor Little Red Riding Hood and her trike for doing the same thing she had done, without even the luxury of a shop.

She swallowed again. This introspection malarkey was more than unpleasant. It was downright dreadful. She could see now why she'd avoided it all her life. It was easier to just keep working, move forward, and stay angry.

"Yoo-hoo? Are you still with us in the land of the living?" Hattie asked, waving her hands animatedly in front of Juliana's face.

I suppose I know where Cherry gets her cartoonish body language from now.

"Yes. Sorry," Juliana said.

Gazing unseeingly into her half-empty mug, she realised she was sorry about a lot of things.

TWENTY

Not Another Moaning Malcolm

CHERRY POUTED at the salad that her mum had placed on the table for lunch. It had been a week of recovering at home, and for the first few days, she had been allowed to eat whatever she liked. Now she was starting to feel better, and with that came salads and far less ice cream.

Luckily, she hadn't broken anything, but she was beginning to suspect that bruising was as painful as broken bones. She'd struggled to take full breaths for the first couple of days which caused her mum to diagnose bruised ribs. Cherry had happily agreed if it meant avoiding a trip to the dreaded doctor.

Slowly but surely, she started to recover. The dizziness faded, the bruises looked less purple, and she regained movement in her limbs. On the fourth day she got out of bed and meandered about the house, feeling lost and purposeless. Every day since then she had spent a little longer out of bed, walking around the house and wondering what she would do next.

Harry was a write-off.

To be honest, Harry had been a breath away from being a write-off when she bought him. Being side-swiped by a lorry was never going to end well for the rust bucket, even if she had painted it pink and assigned it a human identity.

Her insurance premium was going to go through the roof. First a crushed trike, then a concertinaed van. She wondered if she should give it all up. The thought was too painful, so she turned to her meal.

"Salad?" she asked sadly.

"It's healthy."

Cherry lifted a lettuce leaf onto her fork and started to count the halves of cherry tomatoes. As far as she was concerned, they were the only tasty thing in a salad.

"Mum, do you think I should give up on ice cream?"

"No."

Cherry looked up. "Just… no?"

"It's your dream," her mother said. "Always has been. So, you've had a couple of setbacks."

"I nearly died."

"But you're fine."

"Two vehicles have been crushed," she pointed out.

"Which makes it extremely unlikely that it will ever happen again."

"But—"

The house phone rang. Cherry watched her mother jump up from the dining table, swipe up the phone, and smile at the caller ID. "I'll take this in the other room. You eat."

Cherry didn't get a chance to reply. Her mum had already vanished to the living room, closing the door behind her. She narrowed her eyes thoughtfully at the wood panelling. To say that her mother had been acting suspicious since the accident would be an understatement. There were whispered conversations, endless phone calls, and constant trips to the shops, as she claimed they were running out of things that Cherry knew full well they had plenty of.

"Please don't let it be another Malcolm," Cherry whispered.

Of course, she wanted her mum to be happy, and the fact that she felt she needed to hide the fact she was dating was cute, but Hattie Hawkins didn't always pick the best men to date. Moaning Malcolm had been the worst. He'd been boring, complained about everything, and hated ice cream.

"Who hates ice cream, anyway?" Cherry muttered to herself.

The thought of ice cream sent her into a depression again. Harry was gone. She needed to find another vehicle. Maybe this time she'd go with an armoured tank, see if the good people of Wilmsford could manage to crush that.

Or maybe it was time to give up.

Perhaps a nice, safe office job was best. Something with a regular income and practically zero chance of her workplace being flattened. She'd temped as a receptionist in the past, she could do it again. It wasn't a career, or something she would enjoy, but it would be safer than ice cream, which was clearly far more dangerous than she'd ever realised.

She stabbed at a lettuce leaf and twirled it about on her fork. She had no appetite at all. Hadn't felt hungry for a few days. Initially she had comfort-eaten her way through a spectrum of sugar, but now she didn't even want that.

And she certainly didn't want lettuce.

No, she wanted to know what to do next. She wanted answers. Was it time to give up on her dreams?

The door flew open. "You eaten that salad yet?" her mum asked.

Cherry looked at the untouched meal and opened her mouth.

"Never mind. Get your coat on, we're going out."

"Out?" Cherry asked.

"Yes." Her mum dropped the phone back into the cradle and cleared away the uneaten lunch plates.

"Now?" Cherry clarified.

"No, next week. Yes, now. Come on. Chop chop!"

Cherry stood up and dragged herself toward the coat rack in the hall. "If this is to meet another Malcolm, I'll scream."

"What was that?" Her mum shouted from the kitchen.

"Nothing, Mum!"

TWENTY-ONE

Melting Like Sorbet in Sunshine

JULIANA ROLLED UP HER SHIRTSLEEVES. The midday sun burned too hot for her to be wearing a fitted shirt and trousers, but she was doing too much physical work to be at ease in a dress. She'd said as much to Aaron an hour ago, who had suggested she changed into a tank top and a pair of booty shorts, whatever they were. Obviously, she'd levelled with him a glare and told him to go scrub the espresso machine with a toothbrush. It still irked her that he had chuckled good-naturedly while obeying.

Everything irked her today. No, everything stressed her today.

A sweaty delivery man chose that moment to confidently sidle up to her and say, "Hiya, love. It looks like we left a few of the last items back at the depot. No biggie, we'll just pop back and get them now."

Juliana slowly turned to face him. "Is that so?"

His confidence started melting like sorbet in sunshine. "Uh, yeah?"

She took a step closer to him. Her heeled shoes placed them at the same eyelevel and she fixed her gaze on his. "It's *no biggie,* you say?"

"No?"

"You will *just pop back* and get them?"

He shrunk back like a mouse, as scared as if a cat had appeared, but also as confused as if the cat had sprouted two heads. "Yes?"

"Your depot is two counties over! It will take you ages!"

He blinked repeatedly. "No, no. The lads are already on the way and are making good time. They'll be back soon. Besides, the whole set-up looks so good that you'll never notice that everything's not all here."

"I. Better. Not," Juliana said in her deepest, harshest voice.

"Whoa. Well, mark me down as scared *and* horny," said another delivery man behind them.

Juliana spun on her heels until she found the speaker. "What was that?"

"Nothing, Ms Martin-Sinclair," he croaked, avoiding eye contact.

"That's what I thought. If you people spent less time talking behind my back and standing around like misshapen gargoyles, perhaps this could all be finished before our very strict deadline!"

The delivery man who had first spoken nodded hurriedly and called for the others to get back to work.

Juliana waited until they'd gone before opening a box of new supplies. The sun—which was unusually scorching for Britain—wasn't making the work easy. Neither was her desperate need for this to be perfect. Nothing could be allowed to go wrong today.

The back of her neck was starting to burn. She stood to lay her hand over it and ponder if there was any prep she could be doing indoors. There wasn't. And she wasn't the type to shy away from hard work, even if it came with discomfort and useless minions.

With great fury and precision, she thwacked a buzzing fly with a nearby broom. Then she glared at a bird on the roof of the shop until it stopped its infernally cheerful chirping. Silence restored, she returned to ripping open the box. She was just about to dig into its contents when she heard Aaron's voice behind her.

"Juliana? I thought you might need this."

She looked up, ready to bite his head off, and saw him standing there in his ridiculous hipster sunglasses, holding a big mug.

"What's that?"

"It's an iced coffee, or rather an iced triple espresso with some brown sugar."

She snatched the mug. The cold, sweet coffee smell wafted up and mixed with the scent of her perfume and the salty-tang of her heated skin. She closed her eyes and groaned. "You're a life-saver."

He waved that away. "Nah."

"No, really, thank you," she muttered reluctantly, taking her first gulp.

"Well, I was going to bring you some water but figured you need this more. I saw you shouting at those blokes before terrorising the local wildlife and remembered that you hadn't had any caffeine since this morning. Today of all days, we need you sharp, right?"

She was surprisingly moved. There was something special about their relationship, she realised. No matter how prickly and, let's face it—bitchy—she was, he took it in his stride and appeared to understand what was behind her bluster. She wished she had more of those relationships in life. What was it that hadn't alienated him? She'd seen him be pretty bitchy to his friends when they came by to pick him up after work. Maybe he saw it as banter?

"Aaron? Why do you put up with me?"

He shrugged. "Why do you put up with me being late, careless, and usually clueless to what needs to be done in the shop?"

She swigged some coffee. "I'm always too busy to train a new employee?"

He laughed. "There's more to it than that."

She smiled. "Maybe there is."

He nodded at her and began walking back to the shop. Over his shoulder he shouted, "This will all be perfect, you know. You've got this."

Juliana scoffed, not so sure. She drained her mug and set it on the ground before returning to the contents of the box.

TWENTY-TWO

Being Replaced

"STOP MOPING and get out of the car," Hattie ordered.

Cherry rolled her eyes and stepped out of her mother's beaten-up old sports car. She'd gotten a convertible not long after Cherry's father had died, calling it a midlife crisis. It was second-hand and falling apart from day one, but her mum loved it.

It was a gorgeous day, and they'd kept the roof down during the drive into Wilmsford town centre. Cherry's questions about why they were going into town had fallen on deaf ears. She wondered if it was some kind of therapeutic technique her mom had picked up, one where she'd be forced to visit the scene of the accident.

"I really don't want to go into the high street," Cherry complained.

She didn't want to see the corner where her reckless driving had nearly gotten her killed. Nor did she want to see her empty pitch. That would only cause her stress while she continued to wonder if her career in ice cream was over.

"Come on." Hattie walked out of the car park and towards the high street, leaving Cherry no choice but to follow her.

They rounded the corner at the top of the pedestrianised path and started to walk down the slight incline. Cherry remembered riding her trike down the hill on that first day; she'd felt unstoppable. Turned out she could be stopped. Mainly by lorries.

It was unusually busy in the high street, and Cherry wondered if one of the town's many festivals was happening or if she'd gotten her days mixed up and it was a weekend. Some people walked to the side, and through the gap she saw a food truck.

"Wait..." She looked around to double-check what she was seeing. "That... that's my pitch! The council must have given my pitch to someone else. I'm going to kill that... that... that toad!"

"Now, hold on..." Hattie tried.

But it was useless. Cherry was already rushing towards the food truck, fully intent on giving the owner a piece of her mind.

"Excuse me, excuse me," Cherry said as she passed through the crowd to get a better look at the imposter who had taken her place. "Get run over and barely a week later they give your spot to someone else," she muttered.

In front of the food truck were at least a dozen tables, all with chairs neatly tucked underneath them. A condiment station and a waste bin were neatly located beside the pastel blue truck. The shade was her second favourite colour, besides pink, and she found it odd that her replacement had a similar sense of style to her.

"Cherry, you're here!"

She turned to see Juliana rushing from the Gelato Parlour towards her. She wasn't sure why, but somehow Juliana looked… nervous?

"How are you, dear?" Juliana was contemplating her with something that resembled concern.

Dear? Cherry found her attention split between the food truck and Juliana. "I'm… getting better," she admitted. "Good thing I came here when I did."

Juliana's face fell. "You don't like it?"

"Being replaced? No, not much."

Cherry's mum finally caught up to her. "You haven't run off like that since you were a toddler." She placed a hand on her shoulder, leaning forward and trying to catch her breath.

"Do you blame me?" she said. "Look!"

"No, I think *you* should look." Her mum gave her a meaningful stare.

Cherry slowly turned her head and looked at the food truck. It was classy, decorated in light pastels with beautiful script lettering on the side stating that they sold the best ice cream in Wilmsford. The truck wasn't open. It seemed to be in the process of being set up and was already causing a stir of excitement amongst the locals.

"Look up," her mum whispered.

Cherry gazed up at the top of the truck, and a gasp escaped her lips. It was her sign, *Cherry on Top*. She took a step towards the truck and really looked at it. The menu by the side of the serving hatch listed all her ice cream flavours, cold drinks, and more. Even the prices were the same as they'd been on her trike and in Harry.

She turned and regarded Juliana and her mum.

"I'm confused," she admitted.

"It's yours," Juliana said. "And this one is permanent, so at the end of the day you'll lock up and leave it where it is."

"Less chance of it being crushed," her mum added helpfully.

"I…" Cherry looked around in confusion. "My permit is for a non-permanent vehicle only."

"All dealt with," Juliana said.

Cherry didn't know how or why, but she was back in business. She grabbed her mum's face and planted a big kiss on her forehead in celebration. She started to bounce with excitement. She turned and stared at the truck in wonderment.

"I think you better explain everything," Hattie suggested to Juliana.

Juliana nodded and took a small step forward towards Cherry.

"People love your ice cream. Every day since you opened up, customers have been asking me if I stock your flavours. And when I said no, they all gradually flocked to you unless they wanted coffee or cake," Juliana explained. "So, I started thinking about my business model and if I'm really listening to my clientele. You know, giving the people of Wilmsford what they want. And the answer was no. A change was in order."

Juliana pointed to the sign above her shop window. Gone was the *Gelato Parlour* lettering, and, in its place, it read *Cake Parlour*.

"Cake?" Cherry asked.

"Cake." Juliana nodded. "When I look at my last year's worth of sales, I found that it's cake that sells more than gelato. Gelato, sorbet, and ice cream are treats you walk with, or treats you sit outside and enjoy. Coffee and cake are something you enjoy inside."

Cherry wondered if her concussion was back. She was suddenly struggling to catch up. "So, you no longer sell ice cream—or I mean, gelato... you sell cakes?" she clarified.

"That's right," Juliana confirmed.

"Okay. Cool. That still doesn't explain this." She pointed to the food truck behind her.

"It's yours. I know it's no Harry, but I think you'll like it," Juliana said. "It's only two years old, it's had a complete refit recently, and has all the necessary food safety and retail certificates. It's bigger than your previous vehicle, and has another two freezers, which you'll need if you're the only person serving ice cream in town."

Cherry stared at the truck and could only see pound signs in front of her eyes. It must have been expensive, more than she could ever afford.

"Technically, it's mine," Cherry's mum said.

"Indeed," Juliana agreed. "I helped to source and refit it, but your mother owns it. You see, we spoke with your insurance company and, well…"

"They wouldn't give you a bean for Harry," Hattie cut to the chase. "The claims adjustor said it was strange that you'd lost two vehicles so suddenly."

Cherry groaned in frustration. As she suspected, her run of bad luck had cost her any goodwill with her insurer. She frowned as another question popped into her mind.

"But you can't afford this," she said.

"No, but she can." Hattie nodded her head toward Juliana.

Cherry snapped her head over to look at Juliana, whose cheeks were starting to redden.

"We have a deal, a business arrangement," her mum explained. "You'd never get insurance again after all the terrible luck you've had, but I can. So, Juliana has paid upfront for the van, and we've worked out a nice low instalment plan so that you can pay her back. And if anything happens to this van, then Juliana will be able to deal with it. Won't you?"

Juliana quickly nodded. "Absolutely."

"Not that we foresee any issues, do we?" Hattie continued.

"Definitely not, Mrs Hawkins."

Cherry smothered a smirk. It was fun to see Juliana jumpy around her mum.

"What do you think?" Hattie asked.

Cherry took in everything, still in awe of what she was seeing. The truck looked amazing.

"I'm sorry it's not pink," Juliana said. "I couldn't do it. And no eyelashes on the headlights either. I simply couldn't bring myself to do that… to myself."

"It's fine. I love the colour," Cherry confessed.

"Do you want to see inside?" Juliana dangled a key in front of her face.

Cherry nodded gleefully and snatched the key out of Juliana's hand. She rushed over to the truck—she was leaning towards naming this one Gary—and unlocked and opened the back door. She stepped up and inside and marvelled at all the room. It was easily twice as big as Harry had been. She opened freezers and cabinets as she familiarised herself with her new surroundings.

Juliana looked in through the hatch, pensively. "I thought we could share the outdoor seating space? The council were very reticent to allow it, but when I pointed out it would be shared by two businesses, they agreed," she explained.

"On one condition," Cherry said.

Juliana smiled up at her. "Which is?"

"I can stock your sorbets and gelatos."

Juliana agreed. "As long as you don't call them 'snobbish and dull'."

Cherry winced. "Sorry about that. I was angry, I shouldn't have done that."

"I've done far worse," Juliana admitted.

Cherry considered the inside of Gary. "Well, you're certainly making up for it now. Unless this is a long-term strategy to bankrupt both me and my mother?"

Juliana chuckled. "No, let's just say that this made good business sense. You clearly know your business and your customers; you sell out of stock practically every day. I want a piece of that business. And my shop was due for a refresh anyway. I now have more room to stock different types of coffee."

Cherry leaned on the serving hatch and looked down at Juliana with a cheeky smile. "You know, I was thinking about getting into luxury coffees…"

"Don't make me hurt you," Juliana warned with a delicious chuckle.

Cherry was startled by that word, "delicious", popping into her brain. All the same, she leaned into Juliana's teasing with a grin. "Fair enough. Looks like we have a lot to talk about, now that we're business partners."

"Indeed we do. Drinks one night? When you're feeling better, of course. My treat," Juliana suggested.

"I'd like that."

"I'll give you a call." Juliana looked up at her for a couple of moments before she patted the serving hatch counter and took a step back. "Let me know if you need anything," she said before walking away.

Cherry watched her go, unable to help the smile on her face. She bit her lip and turned around to survey the inside her the truck again. Everything had been thought of, and it was all hers. Well, her mum's. And Juliana's? She didn't know the particulars of their business arrangement, but that didn't matter at the moment. She was already thinking about all the product she could fit into a van of this size.

And no more driving, she thought with relief. *No more potentially fatal accidents.*

She'd still not thanked Juliana for driving her home or apologised for dirtying the inside of her car with what was clearly strawberry swirl, not brain matter. She would have to do so later, when they went out for drinks.

It was nice to be on good terms with Juliana. Shouting matches in the middle of the street were hopefully behind them now. She hadn't wanted to push Juliana out of business—she maintained that ice cream and gelato were very different things—but she could understand Juliana's frustration at seeing her business suffering. Cherry would have felt the same way. She hoped they could move onto a new chapter. One as business partners, however that would work.

"Do you like it?" Hattie asked, peering in through

the serving hatch.

"I love him," Cherry admitted.

"Named him already?"

"Gary," she said, then folded her arms. "You know, I thought you were dating someone with all the sneaking around you were doing."

"Not this time," Hattie said. "I knew it would break your heart when you heard about the insurance news, and I didn't want you to give up on your dream."

"Thanks, Mum. I love you."

"I love you, too. Now, you need to focus on getting better and getting back to work. Time is money!"

Cherry laughed. "Wow, you're a harsh taskmaster, huh?"

"Yes, and if you don't listen to me, then I'll send Juliana. Trust me, I've listened to her dealing with enough contractors over the last couple of days to know that she gets things done."

"She certainly does."

"And I think everything will work out with you two now," Hattie said. "Maybe you can be friends... or..."

Cherry raised her eyebrow. "Or?"

"Well. I've seen how you look at each other," Hattie said.

Cherry's jaw dropped. "Wait a minute, how does she look at me?"

Hattie rolled her eyes and turned away.

"Mum, Mum! Wait, I have to lock up... how does she look at me? Mum? Mum!"

TWENTY-THREE

Smash the Toad

THE ESPRESSO MARTINI in Juliana's hand, not to mention the one she'd already downed, wasn't making her feel any better. She was strangely unsettled. Was it due to this newly opened, modern wine bar with all the pretty young things milling about? Or the fact that she hadn't eaten enough today?

Or was it the company?

She sipped her cocktail and watched said company. Cherry was not only all healed up after another week of rest, she had also cleaned up rather nicely for their night out. She was wearing skinny black jeans with a sage-green silk blouse which complemented her reddish-blonde hair. She wasn't wearing makeup, but then with those long eyelashes and that flawless skin, she didn't need to. There were those perfect rosy lips, too.

Wait.

They were moving. Damn it, she'd missed what Cherry was saying.

"Sorry, what was that? I can't hear over the music," she improvised, embarrassed that she had been distracted by Cherry's appearance.

"I said that I like the flavour of this bubble-gum daiquiri. Surprisingly fresh. I bet we could make this into a yummy sorbet if we mixed bubble-gum flavour into some lemon sorbet."

Juliana's breath hitched at the word 'we', but she masked it by taking another sip. "I'll leave the flavours up to you. Past performance shows that I don't know what the public wants in frozen treats, so I'll trust your judgement and stay a silent partner. It's your truck and your flavours."

Cherry looked down at her glass, running her finger around the rim of it. "Yeah, I know. I was just making conversation."

The fidgeting and lack of eye contact told Juliana she wasn't the only one who was uneasy. That made sense. There was so much history between them. How could you be friendly and professional with the person who had made your life a living hell?

She despises me but needs to hide it as we're working together now. Terrific, Juliana realised miserably.

Out loud she said, "So. Your mother told me you have a business degree?"

Cherry perked up. "Yep."

"That explains your skill and intuition for

commerce."

"Thanks," Cherry said, smiling down at her drink. "Oh, you talking to my mum, that reminds me. I wanted to thank you for taking care of me and driving me home. The day when I had my accident, I mean."

"It was the least I could do. After all, it was my behaviour and unseemly screaming that caused you to be reckless in the first place."

Cherry stared at her with wide eyes. "Wait, you're not blaming yourself for that, are you? I was the one who sped off like a maniac in a cute but unreliable rust bucket."

"Yes, that's true. However, I was still responsible for your state of mind." Juliana put her drink down and took a deep breath. "I've given our fight a lot of thought, and I know now that I was wrong. Obviously, your version of events adds up a lot more than what my cynical brain came up with."

"You mean about Colin? Yeah, I'm really not the type to pimp myself out to a douchebag for a permit."

Juliana winced. "I'm sorry for my assumptions. And, if that waste of space did touch you without your permission, then you were right... I was victim-blaming. I don't know how to even start apologising for that."

Cherry shrugged. "It was in the heat of the moment. You were pissed off. It's more important to me what you do now that you have all the facts and you've cooled down."

"Well, now, I'm apologising. From the bottom of my heart. I'm also offering to sever Colin Greene's genitals from his body and force-feed them to him, for you. As a sign of my contrition and support."

Cherry laughed. It was a sound that seemed to warm the already hot bar. It certainly warmed Juliana. She felt her wince melting into a smile.

"No need," Cherry replied. "I don't believe in violence. He called me, you know."

"He did?"

She had gone back to fidgeting with her cocktail glass. "Yep. To check up on me, he said. He even asked to take me out for drinks when I felt better."

Juliana felt a strong aversion to having shared an impulse with Colin the Toad. She, however, had taken Cherry out for drinks because they were discussing business and because she wanted to apologise. Colin had wanted to do it because he was a horny, chauvinist pig without any sense of boundaries. Or any sense of understanding that Cherry was so far out of his league.

Juliana swallowed. "I see. What did you reply?"

Cherry gave her the knowing look that women give each other in these situations. "What do you think? I told him to shove off. I made it clear I wasn't interested in him and added that if he ever touched me, in any way, ever again, I'd make sure everyone knew about it."

"Ah. I bet he took that well," Juliana said, taking another sip of her martini.

Cherry gave a hollow chuckle. "He got all snippy.

He said I should've told him right away that I wasn't into men."

Juliana nearly dropped her glass. "It's true then, you're really not into men? I mean, I recall you saying you weren't straight during our fight but didn't dare to assume that you're a lesbian."

"I'm not. I'm bi. Our little Colin just assumes that any woman who doesn't want to take a ride on his shrivelled disco stick can't like disco sticks at all," Cherry muttered.

"Disco sticks?"

Cherry raised her eyebrows and gave her a meaning look.

"Oh, penises. Right. Yes," Juliana said with a shake of her head, wanting to rid herself of that mental image as quickly as possible. She cleared her throat. "Staying on the unpleasant topic of Colin, I'm glad you told him what would happen if he ever touched you again. However, that isn't enough."

"No? Isn't that up to me to decide?" Cherry said, a warning in her voice.

Juliana checked her tone and choice of words. "I mean that *I don't believe* it is enough. He can't be allowed to get away with behaviour like this. I think you should report him."

Cherry ran her fingers through her unruly hair. "I know. I just... I don't want to get embroiled in something horrible and convoluted. I don't want people to hate me because I cause trouble or to be locked into some big conflict for months on end. I mean, where would I even start?"

Juliana hesitated. Then she opened her handbag and produced a form. She put it on the table in front of Cherry.

She stared at it and then up at Juliana. "Hang on." She snorted out a laugh. "You somehow got your hands on the right form to file a sexual harassment complaint against a council employee. And then just brought it along to a bar?"

Juliana sniffed. "I knew the form, as I had to fill one out a few years ago, so it only took a moment."

"Without checking with me first?"

Juliana squirmed in her seat but tried to look composed. "I'm not saying you have to use it. I only wanted to give you the option."

"Wow. You really do have to control everything, don't you?"

"No, I just—"

She was cut off by Cherry laying her hand on top of her own. "I'm only kidding. Sure, that was a… very Juliana thing to do, but I get why you did it and I'm grateful to have the form."

Juliana stared at their hands. Cherry's fair-skinned one lay confidently on her darker one, as if the gesture was an everyday occurrence for them.

"I-I can help you fill out the form and file it." She returned her gaze to Cherry's. "If you'd like."

"I would." Cherry looked down at the paper and

retracted her hand, as if suddenly shy. "I'm in over my head here."

Juliana sought her gaze again. When she had it, she stated with confidence, "Well, I'm not. At all. As I mentioned, I've done this before, and I want to help you."

"You've been doing a lot of helping me lately," Cherry said, so quiet that her words were barely audible over the bar's music and the other customers' chatter.

"I suppose I have." Juliana sat back and adjusted the shoulder strap of her dress. "Well, it seems to be lowering my blood pressure, so I might as well continue."

"Okay then. Anything to help your health," Cherry said distractedly. She seemed to focus on watching Juliana's hand on the dress strap.

"Oh, it would help my blood pressure immensely to put an end to Colin's appalling and quite frankly criminal behaviour."

Cherry grinned at her, eyes now twinkling. "Then let's smash the douchey toad!"

"Excellent. I'll help you fill in the form tomorrow before work. It's best to do these things sober and well-rested."

Cherry held up her glass in a toast. "It's a deal."

They clinked glasses and drank.

Juliana set her near-empty martini back down. "Anyway, enough about the toad. I want to know what you make of our new setup. Is there anything else you think we need for our shared space?"

Cherry bit her lower lip and then gave a cheeky smile that made Juliana's pulse quicken. "You mean like big, electric-pink umbrellas over every table?"

Juliana tried not to smile back. "I am NOT making my customers drink high-quality espresso under tasteless pink umbrellas."

"Fine. What about the napkins? They can be bright pink, right?"

"Dear, you have your napkins. I have mine. And mine shall remain white with my logo in black. Do whatever the hell you want with yours."

"Hell? You know it's serious when the bad language breaks through the controlled Juliana veneer," Cherry said with another cheeky smile.

Or wait, was that a *flirty* smile? Whatever it was, it caused a buzz in Juliana's stomach, which morphed into heat and radiated lower down.

They watched each other for a beat. The music changed to something slower right as Cherry scooted closer to Juliana on her stool and leaned casually towards her. To a passing stranger they must have appeared to be good friends. Maybe more?

Juliana took a long, deep breath. She still wasn't settled in Cherry's company, but the disquiet had now taken on a new—and much more welcome—tone. As she took in the younger woman's increasingly open body language, complete with that fascinating smile, she reconsidered her assumption that Cherry despised her.

Yes, a totally new tone, she thought. *But what does it mean?*

Juliana gazed at Cherry, though she focused on analysing her own emotions instead. She took a sobering breath and came to an acceptance. There was no longer any doubt. Her bitterness, suspicion, and resentment toward Cherry had vanished. She was left with this muddle of respect, guilt, admiration, and, yes, overwhelming attraction. However, it was so implausible to her that her affection was requited. No matter how Cherry was sitting, acting, or smiling. Juliana was probably reading too much into what was innocent friendliness and Cherry's vivacious body language and personality.

Besides, her crush was futile. She couldn't flirt with Cherry now that she was helping her file charges against someone who'd forced their own attraction onto her. Juliana wasn't going to be equated with Colin the Toad. She and Cherry were working together and cultivating a friendship. That was what she should focus on.

With a sigh, she started to plan her excuse for ending the night early. She had to get home to think this all over and get her bearings. Besides, she had a long day of working with Cherry tomorrow, and she wanted to be at her best for that.

Cherry deserved the best of everything.

TWENTY-FOUR

Without Warning or Permission... Feelings

CHERRY LIFTED the bottle of chocolate sauce and made a pretty criss-cross pattern on top of the large scoop of vanilla ice cream that sat in the waffle cone. Her latest customers were a woman in her mid-thirties and her child. They had just come from Juliana's with an espresso and a small, delicious-looking pastry, which Cherry assumed was for the mother.

The ice cream was clearly for the child who stood on tiptoes, reaching upward to grab the cold treat.

"What do you say?" the mother instructed.

"Thank you!" The kid took the ice cream and quickly applied their tongue to the dripping chocolate sauce.

"You're welcome," Cherry replied with a chuckle.

The child rushed back to their table as the mother paid, thanked Cherry, and also took a seat.

Juliana had been right. Coffees and cakes from one

location, ice creams from another, and a shared space to sit outside in the sun made excellent business sense.

It had been a week since Cherry had returned to work, and she already felt like she'd never been away. All her familiar customers were back, and she'd even acquired some new ones. Having tables seemed to make all the difference. Older and differently abled customers were more likely to order some kind of ice cream snack if it came with a spoon and a place to sit.

Juliana and Aaron seemed to be doing a lot more business, too, if the number of people walking around with takeaway mugs of various caffeinated beverages was anything to go by.

The cooperation between them was working out well. Both businesses were benefitting from it, and Cherry was even enjoying having conversations with someone who was invested—literally and mentally—in what she was doing.

She wiped down the serving counter as her mind drifted back to their drinks at the wine bar the week before. There had been something different about Juliana that night, something intriguing and warm.

They'd spoken a little about business, a little about Cherry's accident, some about getting revenge on Colin, and about Cherry's ideas for new ice cream flavours. But something had still lingered in the air between them.

Something unsaid.

Cherry was pretty sure that Juliana didn't have a

clue. She probably hadn't even noticed the charged atmosphere between them. Cherry had. God, had Cherry noticed it.

At some point, without warning or permission, Cherry had stopped seeing Juliana as the fearsome ice queen who had been trying to put her out of business. Somehow, that had all changed, and Cherry was instead confronted with the caring, gentle Juliana who wanted to help and even protect Cherry.

Cherry would never admit it out loud, not even to herself, but it was an enormous turn-on.

Juliana was *hot*. She had noticed that before, but after the grand gesture Juliana had made, Cherry had started seeing it more. Had started seeing the real Juliana more. She was commanding with her presence and her impressive vocabulary and enjoyed using both to get exactly what she wanted. In the week that they'd worked together, Cherry had enjoyed sitting in on supplier and contractor meetings, watching as Juliana quickly and assertively got what she wanted. It was the kind of behaviour that Cherry enjoyed seeing in a woman, especially a woman she was dating.

While she hadn't been keen to be on the receiving end of those traits, even then she'd half-heartedly wondered if it was an insight into what Juliana might be like behind closed doors. Maybe in the bedroom.

Cherry's cheeks heated up. She coughed and focused her attention on cleaning the bottles of sauce and syrup. She'd been thinking more and more about

Juliana lately, revisiting all the arguments they'd had and understanding that Juliana's anger came from a place of fear. Fear of losing a business which she had worked so hard for.

I would've done the same, she thought. *We're more similar than I realised.*

It wasn't long before her mind drifted back to the crash. On the cold pavement, she had been surprised to open her eyes and be met with Juliana's, even more surprised to find that they were filled with worry. Her soft voice had kept Cherry calm, and there had been no mistaking her care and concern.

Then, that night at the wine bar, Juliana had been bossy but compassionate in her attempts to have Cherry consider a formal complaint against Colin Greene. She hadn't beaten around the bush, but that was Juliana's way. If she had something to say, she said it, but Cherry had come to discover that even Juliana's orders could come from a place of warmth.

A warmth that Cherry was on the receiving end of more and more lately.

Unless I'm reading too much into things?

She sighed and rinsed out the cleaning rag. She had no idea if Juliana would be interested in someone like her. She was young, naïve, liked hot pink and ice cream. Juliana was mature, confident, liked muted colours and strong espresso.

Cherry could see their similarities and how their

differences complemented each other, but that didn't mean that Juliana would.

"Morning, Cherry."

She turned and saw Bob, the local postman, shuffling through a handful of envelopes.

"Morning," she greeted him.

He pulled out three envelopes from the stack and handed them over to her, wished her a nice day, and continued on his rounds.

Cherry's keen eye spotted the council logo on one of the envelopes immediately. She sucked in a breath and held it for a moment. Butterflies smashed against the wall of her stomach as she wondered if it was something about her pitch, her food safety certificates, or her complaint against a well-liked councillor.

The nerves calmed when Cherry reminded herself that Juliana would no doubt be able to deal with whatever the envelope contained.

She tore at the tab, pulling the paper out as soon as she could. She unfolded the letter and skimmed through the details. As she read, her feet moved almost without her knowledge and she found herself on the way to Juliana's shop.

A huge weight lifted from her shoulders. Colin had been dismissed, and the council were apologising for the situation she had been put in. Everything was going to be okay. She was no longer under Colin's control. The toad was done.

She saw Aaron serving customers and assumed

Juliana was in her office in the back of the shop. She sped into the office, closing the door behind her.

Juliana stood by the filing cabinet and offered her a confused frown.

"Are you okay?" she asked with concern.

Cherry was more than okay. She was elated. She grabbed hold of Juliana's face and lowered her head to apply a solid kiss to the woman's forehead. It was a move she'd done a hundred times before with her parents, her family, and her friends.

But never with Juliana.

And in the next second, she realised that fact.

TWENTY-FIVE

Wild Intoxication

JULIANA FELT the soft hands cupping her face. Then the heat of Cherry's breath and body as she drew closer. She saw Cherry's rosy lips form a kissing shape.

Gods above, she's going to kiss me!

That was when Juliana's brain shut off and her body took over. There was only one thing she wanted right now. That kiss. In one swift move she lifted her head, her lips brushing into the gentlest connection with Cherry's.

When Cherry had rushed into her office, Juliana had been worried since she had run in with such urgency, but she'd also been so pleased. Cherry's presence was a pick-me-up stronger than any espresso. Now, in that split second in which their lips were pressed together, that pick-me-up was ramping up into a wild intoxication. Juliana's head was swimming, her body was buzzing hot with arousal and affection, and her mouth wanted more of Cherry. She was aware that she was pushing her lips harder against Cherry's, which were colder than hers from the outside air, and also noticed that Cherry had stepped even closer into her own personal space.

Then, a realisation came to her, like ice water trickling down her spine. This wasn't the way she did things.

She pulled away. Cherry gave a disappointed little whimper as she did so, making Juliana hurry to explain her actions.

"I apologise for stopping the kiss. Which was marvellous, by the way." She paused to give Cherry a shaky, though hopefully reassuring, smile. "Nevertheless, I was raised to do things properly. You can call me old-fashioned, but I prefer to save the kissing until I've been on a date or two with a woman. With that in mind, I—"

Cherry held up a hand. "I've gotta stop you right there." She hooked her lower lip with her teeth and there was something like pity in her eyes. "That, um, wasn't meant to be that sort of kiss. I mean it was nice, really nice. But I need to be honest with you, I only meant to kiss your forehead."

Humiliation pushed out every other sensation that had been flooding Juliana's senses. How could she have been so foolish? So pathetic? So uncontrolled?

TWENTY-SIX

Explanations

CHERRY WANTED TO KICK HERSELF. Obviously, Juliana was completely unaware that Cherry's celebratory move was to kiss someone on the forehead. No normal person did that. But then, Cherry had never been accused of being normal.

"My… forehead?" Juliana whispered.

She had the look of someone who was crushed and mortified and failing miserably to appear unaffected.

"It's stupid," Cherry continued. "I… I do that when I'm happy. When I have something to celebrate. I just get so excited that I…" She trailed off, miming the action of taking someone and applying a kiss to their forehead. "I'm grabby."

"Grabby. I see." Juliana turned away and retreated behind her desk. Her cheeks were flushed. Cherry felt terrible for causing her such embarrassment.

Suddenly, her brain caught up.

Juliana had *kissed* her. And then asked her on a *date*.

And Cherry had ruined everything by opening her stupid mouth.

"I'd love to go out with you," she said.

Juliana's gaze shot up from her paperwork. "Is that a joke?" Her body language seemed to show less embarrassment now. It had moved onto anger instead. At least that was an emotion Cherry had seen in Juliana before, one she could work with.

"No. I wouldn't joke about—"

"What were you so happy about anyway?" Juliana asked, taking a seat and focusing on a piece of paper which couldn't possibly need as much attention as it was receiving.

"The council have fired Colin," she quickly explained. "He's gone and they've formally apologised. I wanted to tell you… to thank you."

"I see." Juliana jerked her head in an uncomfortable nod. "Well, congratulations. That's good news."

Cherry knew she needed to fix this swiftly, or there would be a cloud hanging over them for who knew how long. She snatched the piece of paper out of Juliana's hand and placed it face down on the desk.

"I was reading that," Juliana groused.

"I'm sorry—"

"We don't need to have this conversation. You should return to work. As should I." Juliana reached for another piece of paper.

Cherry grabbed all of the stray paper from Juliana's

desk and placed it on a spare chair. "You said you were raised to do things properly," she said. "Well, so was I. I wasn't raised to burst into someone's office and kiss them without asking for their permission, even if that person is insanely hot and even if I'd like nothing more than to kiss them. I didn't want you to think that I'd do that. Consent, it's important to me, you know?"

Juliana stared up at her, confusion etched into her features.

"I had to be honest with you, but I didn't want to hurt you. I just, didn't want us to start off on a lie. I didn't want us to be telling our grandchildren about our first kiss and it be based on a lie."

"Grandchildren?" Juliana spluttered.

"Not that I'm rushing ahead, it was just to make a point!" Cherry started to pace the office, wishing that she was better at explaining herself. She hadn't prepared anything to say, but now she felt she needed to be brave and admit her feelings. If she didn't, the misunderstanding between them would be left to fester and the closeness she'd been enjoying would evaporate.

"I like you," she blurted out. "Like, a lot. But I didn't think you'd like me. And then you kissed me, which was amazing, by the way. And I sort of wish I hadn't said anything, so we could've carried on kissing, but I had to be honest with you. And if the offer of that date is still on the table…"

Juliana cleared her throat before she nodded, and Cherry's heart soared.

"I'm sorry I manhandled you," Juliana said softly.

"You didn't." Cherry shook her head. "Anyone would've made the assumption you did. The forehead kiss thing, I do it with people I'm close to. And I kinda feel close to you."

"I feel close to you, too," Juliana confessed.

"So, we'll start over," Cherry decided. "No one kissed anyone. We'll go on a date and see what happens from there, right?"

Juliana smiled. "That sounds like a good idea. I'll pick you up tonight. Is seven okay?"

"Seven is perfect. I look forward to it," Cherry said. She remembered that she had left her ice cream truck abandoned and hoped the locals weren't raiding the wafers. "You know where to find me."

She opened the door and walked back into the shop, grateful for the wave of air conditioning that cooled her heated cheeks. She knew she'd be in a daze the rest of the day, but it would be worth it.

She had a date with Juliana Martin-Sinclair.

TWENTY-SEVEN

Her Neglected Heart

THERE WAS no way Juliana was eating something called a 'mighty meat stack with cheesy piggy'. She would rather eat a dead skunk's tail.

"Go on," Cherry urged. "Try it. I had it when this place opened, and it's easily the best bacon cheese-burger in Wilmsford!"

Juliana fought the urge to groan. Why had she let Cherry pick the restaurant for their date? Right now, she could be seated in the tasteful ambiance of Le Merveilleux, sipping a vintage wine while waiting for her confit de canard. Instead, she was in the new burger place by the cinema. Squeezed into a hard, plasticky booth. With a sticky table. While some song about milkshakes bringing boys to yards blared through several speakers.

There was a cutting reply on her tongue, but she kept it there when she saw how delightedly Cherry was perusing the menu. When Cherry smiled like that, not to mention when her eyes lit up like that, Juliana was helpless. She resigned herself to her fate and scanned the menu for something edible. There was a chicken burger with side salad. That would have to do.

She put her menu down and relished in watching Cherry read the print off the menu while humming and swaying along to the music. Suddenly the redhead's delight changed to something more like frustration.

"Ah! I can't decide," Cherry whinged. "Should I get the 'mighty meat stack with cheesy piggy' or the 'bison burger with a kick'?"

"Why not order both and eat half of each? As I said, tonight is my treat. Have whatever you want."

Cherry stared at her, eyes widening. "I can have both? Two meals?!"

Juliana smiled. "Have three. Live a little."

"No. That's bonkers," Cherry said while inspecting their table. "Three plates wouldn't fit. I'll have two, though. If you're sure?"

"Positive."

Cherry fretted with her blouse sleeve. "I don't know. It's a lot of food waste."

"Then ask them to box your leftovers up so you can bring them home for tomorrow."

"Ooh, clever!"

Juliana quirked an eyebrow and deadpanned, "Yes, I'm a veritable mastermind."

Cherry ignored the comment and turned the menu over. "What are you drinking?"

"I don't know. Water?"

Cherry scrunched her face up. "On a date?"

"It's not what I'd normally have on a date, but then neither is a 'cluck-cluck burger', dear." Juliana nodded towards the title of her meal.

Cherry laughed. "I guess not. I'm sorry for bringing you here, Juliana. I know it's not very romantic. I just…" She looked down. "Wanted to be comfortable. You're so bloody formidable, and sometimes it makes me feel a bit, well, inferior. So, I guess I picked this place to compensate."

Juliana adjusted the strap of her black Chanel sheath dress, suddenly wishing she'd worn something more casual. "You should never feel inferior. Not around anyone, but especially not around me. We're different, but that doesn't mean one of us is more correct than the other."

"It's easy for you to say that. It's not as easy for me to feel it," Cherry mumbled, fidgeting with her blouse sleeve again. She looked as uncomfortable in her own skin as she did in that wrinkly and far-too-tight blouse. It made Juliana's heart ache.

Silence fell and lasted for a few tense moments.

Juliana plucked up the courage to sacrifice her pride. Anything to make Cherry feel better. "Would it help if I admitted that I'm dreadfully nervous?"

Cherry looked up. "You're nervous, too?"

"Of course I am. I'm on a date with a charming, fascinating, and absolutely stunning younger woman. Don't you think I feel that you're out of my league as well?"

When Cherry didn't answer, Juliana added, "It doesn't help that I'm still swimming with guilt over how I treated you. The things I did to you, the things I said to you. Everything."

Now it was Juliana's turn to fidget. She picked up a napkin and started folding and unfolding it. She was embarrassed and out of her comfort zone. As always when she experienced feelings she couldn't deal with, she morphed them into anger. Suddenly, she was irrationally infuriated. She made an effort to control it but failed.

"That again? That's all in the past," Cherry said with a dismissive wave. "I understand where you were coming from and don't blame you at all." A crooked smile tugged at one corner of her beautiful lips. "Besides, I have to admit, you're really hot when you go off like that."

Juliana tried to let that compliment douse her anger. "Thank you. I've always been temperamental. Thankfully, I'm not the only one with that trait in my family, so my parents knew how to deal with it."

"Oh, so the hot temper runs in the family?"

"Yes." Juliana dropped the napkin and pointed at Cherry. "But the temper comes from my English side.

Not the Latin one, so you can forget all about the fiery Latina stereotype!"

Cherry held up her hands. "Whoa! Okay! Cease fire. I'm not the enemy anymore, remember? Not that I'd say something that stereotypical even if we were still busy with our, you know, our…" She gestured with her hand in the air as if fishing for the right term before finally settling on, "Our ice cream war."

Juliana forced herself to take a deep breath and rubbed her forehead. "No, of course not. I apologise for the outburst. Anger is my standard outlet when emotions run high."

"Oh." There was a shift in the mood as Cherry glanced up at her through long eyelashes. "And what emotions are running high right now?"

That look and the tone of Cherry's voice, all of a sudden vulnerable but suggestive, made Juliana weak in the knees.

Thank goodness she was sitting down.

"I… think you know. That accidental kiss in my office must have told you everything you needed to know about how I feel."

A lock of hair fell out of Cherry's top knot and, oh so slowly, caressed its way down her cheek. Juliana envied it. Cherry was still giving her that look, making her weaker by the second. Juliana's hands itched to reach out and touch the beauty sitting across from her.

"It did," Cherry said in a rasping voice. "I'd still like you to tell me, Juliana. Use all those fancy words that you keep in that sharp mind of yours. You wanted to go on a date to woo me, so… do it. Woo me."

Juliana's heart pounded like it wanted to break free of her ribcage. She had the strangest sensation of being the hunter and the prey at the same time. How the hell could she feel like *this* in a tacky, yellow-walled, fluorescent-lit, burger joint?

"Hello there!" A cheerful waitress suddenly appeared by Juliana's side. "Sorry to interrupt. Can I get you started off with some drinks?"

Juliana found the instinct to throttle the waitress nearly irresistible. As if she knew this, Cherry reached over and placed her hand on Juliana's. It could have been condescending if it had been someone else, but not with this earnest and kind woman. Cherry's thumb caressed circles on the back of Juliana's hand. It made her rage ebb away to make room for the return of her earlier arousal and affection.

"Hi," Cherry said to the waitress. "Can we get whatever lager you've got for me and a glass of white wine to go with this pretty lady's chicken burger?"

Juliana was so used to stepping up in these situations and ordering that her mouth fell open in surprise. Only for an instant, of course.

She was about to get involved but then checked herself. What was the point? Why did she have to be in control all the time? Cherry could take care of this. Juliana sat back and relaxed while her date engaged the waitress in polite small talk. Juliana simply kept her focus on Cherry's soft hand holding hers, only dialling back into the conversation when Cherry answered whether they were ready to order food with a confident "Yep!" Then she spun to face Juliana. "Ah, man, I did it again. Why do I always charge right into things?" She slapped her forehead with her free hand. "I promised myself I'd pay more attention to your point of view and your wishes. Sorry! Are we ready to order, Juliana?"

"Yes, dear," Juliana said, amused at how sheepish Cherry looked and how affectionate her own voice had sounded.

"Cool. Can I get the 'mighty meat stack with cheesy piggy' and the 'bison burger with a kick', please? Both with sweet potato fries," she said to the waitress before turning back to Juliana. "And it was the cluck-cluck burger you wanted right? With a side salad?"

Juliana felt her smile go from ear to ear. "Clearly you know exactly what I want and need. Carry on."

Cherry's posture relaxed and she smiled back at Juliana, showing bright teeth to match her glittering eyes. The waitress was completely forgotten until she cleared her throat and said, "So, um, can I get you two lovebirds any starters?"

Juliana's breath hitched at the word 'lovebirds'. Could *love* be budding between her and Cherry? Could someone like Cherry ever love her?

She looked at their hands, still clasped on the table,

and her neglected heart beat harder as she dared to hope.

It was hours later, when the eatery was closing, that Juliana and Cherry agreed to leave. Juliana noticed an ache in the pit of her stomach at the thought of the date ending. They had spent hours chatting, long enough for Cherry to get through both her burger meals and then a brownie, which was served with whipped cream. They'd decided to stay away from ice cream since they weren't meant to be talking about work.

The evening had been something special. Fun, romantic, relaxing, and thrilling, all in one. Now that was coming to an end, and Juliana wished she could stop time.

They ambled, side by side, toward her car. It was only then that Juliana remembered she'd drunk two glasses of the diner's terrible, cheap house wine. She was so used to walking home or taking a taxi after a late dinner that she'd completely forgotten she had picked Cherry up in the Mercedes. That presumably meant she would have to drive them home.

"Cherry, I'm frightfully sorry," she said with a croak. "I had wine. I can't drive."

"I know. I assumed we'd walk," Cherry said, still keeping up the pace and looking ahead, perfectly relaxed.

"Walk? That would take an age and a half! We're on the opposite side of town from your mother's house!"

Cherry let her hand brush Juliana's before taking it. "Yeah, but we're not too far away from your flat, right?"

There was no mistaking the sensual tone of voice, nor the insistent fingers interlacing seductively with her own. They brought up images of intertwining legs in Juliana's mind.

"Cherry, I…"

"You were raised to do things properly and don't jump into bed with women on the first date? Yeah, I know. I had to try, though. You're pretty irresistible, you know?" Cherry said, using a coy free hand to tuck a wisp of hair behind her ear.

Seeing Cherry's shyness, Juliana's composure returned. "So are you. Be that as it may, you deserve better than to be hastily seduced after the first date, especially one of greasy burgers and beer." She sought Cherry's gaze. "I want to get to know you better and get a chance to treat you like a queen before we take things any further."

"Hang on. 'Any further'? What exactly does that mean, Juliana? Are we talking sex or, like, kissing?"

Juliana raised her eyebrows, as much in surprise as in confusion. "You want me to specify details?"

Even in the dim glow of the streetlights, she could see Cherry blush. "No, I meant… Or rather I mean, that I get that you want to wait to sleep with each other. But you know, a first kiss—a non-accidental one this time —might be nice."

Juliana felt as if she'd been given a shot of brandy straight to her heart. "Yes. However, *nice* is not the word I'd choose. I'd say that kissing you would be," she paused and breathed out the final word, "sublime."

Cherry nodded quickly and repeatedly. Juliana could see her throat bob as she swallowed. That tight blouse strained over her chest as she took deep, swift breaths. She looked vulnerable, probably as startled by what was happening between them and the speed of it as she herself was.

Juliana made herself pause and take stock. Cherry's nervousness spoke of feelings as surprisingly deep as her own. How had this all been growing between them while they were busy fighting? How had they not noticed how perfect they could be together? Cherry's hand was heating up in Juliana's.

This… this was the moment Juliana should take full control of the situation. It was up to her to steer this right, for both of them. She knew it with the same certainty that she knew she was falling head over heels for this woman.

She stopped and, connected by their hands, made Cherry stop, too. She gently manoeuvred Cherry toward a wall and made sure she was comfortably leaned against it before moving closer. Then even closer. In her heels she was taller than Cherry, so she craned her neck a little until her mouth was a hair's breadth away from those rosy lips. Juliana could faintly smell chocolate brownie on Cherry's hot breath and feel her hands clasp her waist, holding on for dear life.

Juliana parted her lips ever so slightly to connect them with Cherry's and then, finally and firmly, kissed her. Cherry's body quivered, and she moaned against Juliana's lips. There were so many ways their mouths could fit together. They tried them all, each one ravenous for the other.

Juliana had wanted time to stop before. Now it felt as if it really did.

This was the way she'd always wanted to kiss a lover, the way she knew she would always want to be kissed. There was more than lust and need in this. There was real, deep emotion. Her heart, her mind, and her every sense were filled with Cherry, and yet it wasn't enough. How could anyone taste and smell as delicious, feel as good, and kiss as well as this woman?

Cherry's hands now moved from Juliana's waist, and her own hands moved from where they'd been planted on the wall on either side of Cherry. As if by unspoken agreement, their hands found each other and held on tight. Their bodies pressed closer. Breasts to breasts. Hips to hips. Very slowly, Cherry parted her lips fully to take Juliana's tongue inside her mouth and caress it with her own.

As their fingers entwined, Cherry moaned again, more sweet than sexual this time. It was more like a whimpering sigh, and it shot straight into Juliana's pounding heart.

She slowly extricated herself from the kiss to whisper, "What have you done to me, Cherry Hawkins?"

"I don't know," Cherry panted. "I don't know what you've done to me either. Whatever it is, I want it every night from now on."

"Every night and every day," Juliana agreed, gazing into Cherry's heavy-lidded eyes.

"Well, that's it then," Cherry mumbled. "The ice cream war ends with not only a ceasefire but a coalition."

Juliana took a step back and quirked an eyebrow. "A coalition? No, my sweet, I won and conquered you."

Cherry snorted. "Trust me, General Control Freak, it takes more than this to *conquer* me."

"Really? Pray tell me what it'll take," Juliana bantered back.

Cherry's shyness returned. "You said it yourself: moments like this one, happening every night and every day from now on."

There was no stopping the smile that spread from Juliana's heart to her face. "Now that is a peace treaty I can live with." She gave Cherry a quick kiss on the lips and added, "Now, let's call a taxi. Dear Hattie Hawkins will kill me with her laser vision if I don't have you home at a decent time."

Cherry laughed. "You can't blame Mum for that. All's fair in love and war!"

Reviews

We sincerely hope you enjoyed reading Ice Cream Wars.

If you did, we would greatly appreciate a short review on your favourite book website.

Reviews are crucial for any author, and even just a line or two can make a huge difference.

About the Author

A.E. Radley had no desire to be a writer but accidentally turned into an award-winning, best-selling author.

She has recently given up her marketing career and position as Managing Director in order to make stuff up for a living instead. She claims the similarities are startling.

She describes herself as a Wife. Traveller. Tea Drinker. Biscuit Eater. Animal Lover. Master Pragmatist. Annoying Procrastinator. Theme Park Fan. Movie Buff.

Connect with A.E. Radley
www.aeradley.com

The Road Ahead

Two women from very different backgrounds. Forced to share a long journey home. Will they work together or pull each other apart?

Rebecca is stuck in Portugal. All planes to England are grounded and it's only two days until Christmas.

Desperate to get home but without money to hire a car; she's stuck. She sees an opportunity when she meets a snobby businesswoman with a broken leg, a platinum credit card, and a desire to get home. A tentative agreement is struck in order reach their destination before the festive deadline. Will they make it, or will they kill each other along the way?

A heartwarming enemies to lovers romance with a twist. Discover The Road Ahead and make your own journey home today.

The Road Ahead | Preview

BY A.E. RADLEY

"EXCUSE ME! SORRY!"

Rebecca rushed past an elderly couple. She looked at her watch and started to run towards the terminal building. Time was running out. She had to catch her flight, she couldn't afford to miss it. Around the corner, she almost collided with another elderly couple.

Apparently, the Algarve was full of them. Slowly meandering around, not caring if they were in the way. Usually appearing to be in a world of their own. They eyed her with confusion, probably wondering what the fuss was about. The concept of time seemed to be lost on most of them.

"Sorry!" she called over her shoulder as she side-stepped them and sprinted towards the airport entrance.

She knew she shouldn't have relied on the taxi service her hotel recommended. It seemed a little too much of a coincidence that the lazy receptionist shared a surname with the taxi driver. When he'd finally turned up, he seemed less interested in getting to the airport and more interested in his telephone call. So much so that they missed the turn to the airport, adding to the delay.

The automatic doors parted, and she entered the building. She slowed her running to a jog, looking around in confusion. The departures terminal was packed with people standing around. Angry-looking people. Arms were folded, and a combined murmuring of displeasure filled the air. Something was definitely up.

Rebecca took a few steps forward and looked up at the ceiling monitors. Her eyes widened. Each and every flight on the departure board was marked as delayed.

"No, no, no," she whispered to herself.

A businessman was standing beside her, looking at his phone and shaking his head.

Rebecca turned towards him. "Excuse me, do you know what's happening?"

He looked up. "Some massive computer failure. Knocked out air traffic control in all of Portugal and Spain. Everything is grounded."

Rebecca swallowed. "Everything?" She removed her heavy backpack and lowered it to the floor.

He nodded. "Yeah, speak to a check-in assistant, but that's what they told me." He held up his phone for her to see the screen. "And that's what the news says."

"Did they say how long it would be?" Rebecca felt cold fear grip at her. She had to get home, she didn't have time for delays.

"No idea, could be ten minutes, could be ten hours. Personally, I don't think it will be that long. It can't be." He lowered his phone and gestured to the growing crowd. "This close to Christmas, they'll be calling everyone in to get it sorted out."

Rebecca looked around at the people in the departure hall. In her mind, people and planes were like water and glasses. Water spilt from a glass always looked like so much more compared to water contained in one. It was the same with people. Sat on a plane, the number of people looked reasonable, but sprawled out in an airport, they seemed like enough to fill hundreds of flights.

She turned back to the businessman. He looked authoritative, some kind of higher-up executive, she assumed. In her experience, people like that didn't always have the best grasp on reality. They assumed that their personal assistant, faithful Marjorie, would fix everything in a jiffy. They didn't know that Marjorie had sold her kidneys, killed a man, and bribed law officials to do what needed to be done because she had a large mortgage, three children, and a beagle, and needed her job whatever the cost.

"Thanks," she said. She picked up her bag and made her way through the crowds to the check-in desks.

The long row of desks was manned by exhausted-looking staff who seemed to be struggling to maintain a customer-facing smile. Luckily, there were no queues. Most people had given up speaking to the airline staff and were now standing around looking discontent, delivering filthy looks to any staff member who made eye contact.

Hoping against hope, Rebecca walked towards a free desk.

"Hi, Rebecca Edwards," she introduced herself to the woman. She took her passport and her boarding pass from her pocket and handed them over. "I'm due to fly to Heathrow, but I hear there is a delay?"

"All flights are delayed at the moment. There is a computer problem and no flights can land or take off." The woman didn't even make a move to pick up her passport or boarding pass.

"Right," Rebecca said. She chewed her lip. "Any idea of time?"

"As soon as we hear anything, it will be announced over the speaker and on the screens." The woman pointed up towards the screens that hung from the ceiling.

"Okay..." Rebecca knew that there was nothing more to be done, but she couldn't bring herself to walk away from the desk. She lowered her heavy bag to the floor again, her mind racing as she wondered what to do next.

The illogical part of her felt that standing around the check-in desk would somehow help her predicament. The desk was a critical part in the whole boarding process. Somehow, being there gave her hope. But in her heart, she knew it was futile.

"I'm sorry, there really is nothing I can do." The check-in assistant offered an apologetic smile.

"I really need to get home," Rebecca said. She leaned on the high check-in desk, pushing aside a stand-up marketing message regarding the airline's award-winning customer service. "When do you think the next plane will leave?"

"I'm sorry, but I don't have any information to give you." The assistant, Beatriz if her nametag was to be believed, tapped some buttons on her keyboard while squinting at the screen.

"I know it's not your fault," Rebecca added.

She watched as an irate German woman yelled at the poor check-in assistant beside her. She'd never understand how someone could be so mean, especially to the people on the front line. Yes, the airport had a massive computer failure. Yes, planes were grounded. Yes, it was the twenty-third of December. But that was no reason to take it out on the minimum wage check-in assistants.

"Sorry about all the people shouting at you, it must really suck," Rebecca said. She knew she didn't have to apologise for someone else's behaviour, but she wanted to.

The German woman left, blasting out obscenities as she went.

"It is a busy time of year," Beatriz replied. "Many people want to get home. The air traffic control systems have been down since early this morning, and we have no idea when they will be back up and running. It isn't just Faro Airport that's affected, it's many airports throughout the country. And in Spain, too."

"Must be horrible for you to have to deal with it," Rebecca sympathised. She fretted with her hair tie. She couldn't imagine having to tell hundreds of irate passengers that news, over and over again.

"In all my years of flying, I've never seen such incompetence!"

Rebecca winced at the British voice. She turned to look at who had taken over from the German woman to be in the running for rudest passenger of the morning.

The woman was approximately in her forties and wore a black skirt suit. Her long, blonde hair was perfectly styled in soft curls that fell to her shoulders. Rebecca glanced down at the woman's feet, noting a plaster cast on one foot, which looked at odds with the business attire. For a brief second, she wondered what had happened and felt a pang of sympathy towards her.

"I need to get back to London, now. How are you

going to make that happen?" the woman demanded. She smacked her passport onto the check-in desk.

Rebecca's eyes widened at the tone. Her sympathy at the woman's cast evaporated. She turned back to Beatriz.

"Wow," she whispered and tilted her head towards the loud woman. "Rude."

Beatriz smiled and nodded in agreement.

"Don't know why she's complaining, she should fly her broom home," Rebecca muttered.

Beatriz chuckled. She looked thoughtfully at Rebecca for a moment. She leaned forward, gesturing for Rebecca to do the same.

Rebecca stood on her tiptoes and pivoted forward. She wondered why airport check-in desks were often so high. She was hardly short, but even she struggled to see over them sometimes.

"There were two planes to London due before yours," Beatriz explained, gesturing around the busy airport.

Rebecca turned around. She regarded the angry passengers standing around, most of them shaking their heads. The occasional tut could be heard.

"I can't say when the computer system will be up and running, but even if it sprang to life right now, the two planes from this morning would take priority. We don't have enough planes to take everyone today, and we can't divert from other airports as it's so close to Christmas."

Rebecca's heart rate picked up as she began to understand the reality of the situation.

"All of the other airlines will be fully booked," Beatriz concluded.

"You're telling me that my chance of getting home for Christmas is bad, right?" Rebecca guessed.

Beatriz nodded. "By plane, yes."

Rebecca frowned. "Is there another way? What about the trains?"

"Altogether impractical, miss. To travel from Faro to London, you would have to get to Lisbon, then take a night train to the Spanish-French border. Then, you'd have to switch to travel to Paris, and then switch again for the high-speed rail to London." The assistant frowned as if to emphasise her point. "A lot of transfers, and it could be expensive."

Rebecca's heart sank. "Not to mention the timing. I'd never get home for Christmas."

Something about her plight must have resonated with Beatriz. The woman gestured for Rebecca to come a little closer. She did the best she could, standing on the very tips of her Converse All-Stars. "Very soon, these people are going to realise that time is running out, and they are going to look for alternative methods of transport. You can, technically, drive to London and get home for Christmas. But there will be a limited number of cars available for hire…"

The penny dropped. Rebecca slowly nodded as she

understood. Beatriz smiled, picked up Rebecca's passport and boarding pass, and handed them back to her.

"I'm sorry, Miss Edwards, there's nothing I can do," she said loudly.

"Thank you, thank you so much," Rebecca whispered as she grabbed the items and hoisted her rucksack onto her shoulder.

"You better hurry," Beatriz advised quietly.

"I will, thank you again," Rebecca said. She turned and looked at the airport signage, searching for a pictogram of a car and her way home.

About the Author

Emma Sterner-Radley, a Swedish romance and fantasy writer, got a degree in Library and Information Science because she wanted to work with books, and being an author was an impossible dream, right? Wrong. She's now a writer and a publisher. (But still a librarian at heart.)

She lives with her wife and two cats in England. There's no point in saying which city, as they move about once a year. She spends her time writing, reading, daydreaming, exercising, and watching whichever television show has the most lesbian/sapphic subtext at the time.

Her weaknesses are coffee, sugary snacks and small chubby creatures with tiny legs.

www.emmasternerradley.com

Life Pushes You Along

Zoe's on autopilot. Rebecca is stagnating. When change comes knocking, will they open the door?

Twenty-something Zoe Achidi feels safe in her unchallenging life in a London bookshop. Bored, but safe.

Her only excitement comes from pining over frequent customer, Rebecca Clare, unobtainable as this beautiful businesswoman in her forties seems.

One day, Zoe's brother and her best friend bring Zoe and Rebecca together.

While they connect, and it turns out Rebecca is also bored with her life, their meetings remain all business. When things take a turn for the worse, life pushes along.

But will Zoe and Rebecca end up being thrust in the same direction?

If you're looking for an age-gap romance that will inspire you to shake up your life, then look no further.

Take the leap with Life Pushes You Along by Emma Sterner-Radley

CHAPTER ONE

ZOE WATCHED as one of her favourite customers observed her with what seemed to be desperation. She felt her heart twinge with sympathy.

"So, do you have it?" he asked.

She knew she was going to disappoint him.

"I'm not sure, Mr. Evans. A book with a bird on the cover that was based somewhere with a big forest... that doesn't ring a bell, I'm afraid."

The bookshop's unpleasantly sharp fluorescent lights showed every crease on his wrinkled face as it took on an embarrassed look.

Zoe quickly added, "I know the feeling though. There's lots of books I have been looking for and I can't remember anything but the cover, or a piece of the plot, or half of the author's name. It's a pain."

He nodded. "Yes. Yes, my dear, it certainly is."

"Do you remember anything else about the book? Who was the main character?"

He looked up at the ceiling for a moment. "I suppose she was quite a bit like you, actually."

Zoe felt her brow furrowing. She didn't want to be rude but that didn't narrow it down much. Did he, perhaps, mean that the main character was someone who worked with customers, someone who dressed like her, or someone who was in their late twenties? She hoped he wasn't alluding to the fact that she wasn't white because she wasn't sure if a conversation with this elderly gentleman would stay politically correct if they got onto that subject. She liked Mr. Evans and wanted to continue liking him.

"I see. Um, how was she like me?"

"Young and likable," he answered simply.

Zoe was relieved. It was still just as impossible to find the book he was looking for, though.

"I'm afraid that doesn't give me much to go on. Tell you what, I'll keep an eye out for a book with a forest setting and a bird on the cover. We have your contact details on file, so I can call you if we get it in?"

His face lit up. "That would be splendid! Thank you ever so much for your help."

She smiled at him, happy to be able to help. Mr. Evans put his trilby hat back on, and she couldn't help but smile at his posh, old-fashioned sense of style which perfectly matched his way of speaking.

"Goodbye. I hope to hear from you but if I do not, I shall come in to purchase another book instead."

"You do that, Mr. Evans. Goodbye."

Just as he was leaving the bookshop, he turned around and shouted, "Oh, by the way, it might have been something other than a bird, now that I think about it. I think it was something that flew. So, maybe t'was a bat, a moth, or perhaps a ferret? Anyway, cheerio."

The door closed behind him and Zoe stared into space, puzzled.

Had he meant to say 'ferret'? How the hell was that categorized as something that flew?

Zoe's manager, and the owner of the bookshop, Darren, walked in with a small box under one arm.

He held out the box to her. "We've got a book delivery. Who was that?" He inclined his head towards the door.

"Oh, it was Mr. Evans."

Darren's bushy eyebrows met at the bridge of his nose. "Who?"

"Mr. Evans. You know, the retired bank manager who likes books about nature and sea journeys. Comes in here every week?"

Darren still looked like he was trying to do complicated arithmetic.

Zoe managed not to sigh. "The old guy with the big mole on his right cheek?"

"Oh, that crazy, posh old badger. Right. Anyway,

here's the new batch. Put them on the system and then shelve them, will you?"

She gave a curt nod and took the box from him. There was no reason why he couldn't do this himself–well there was one reason and that was simply that he was lazy. He'd stand at the counter and watch her put the books out, and as soon as she was done he'd slink back into the breakroom, leaving her to man the counter as always, while he drank his bodyweight in sweet tea. *No wonder he always needs to use the loo*, she thought as she unpacked the books. She put them on the system and looked at the packing slip to check the details as she did so.

Her job wasn't the dream that most other book-nerds conjured up when she told them what she did. Yes, she worked in an independent bookshop. However, it was a lacklustre bookshop, where she was overworked, her boss didn't care much about the running of the place, and the clientele was dwindling.

As Zoe began to shelve the books, she looked around at the cheap birch bookcases, faded beige walls, and harsh fluorescent lights and thought about how she had ended up here.

She had been in dire straits when she applied for this job. She had been out on the street since her parents kicked her out. She didn't think she was focused enough for further education, she was down to her last twenty pounds and totally unqualified for any job.

Out of desperation, she had applied for this position and when Darren had asked her, in the interview, why he should hire her and not the other two applicants, who both had degrees and experience, she had broken down in tears. He had grumbled about not being able to stand seeing people cry and after a long chat about her situation, he had agreed to give her the job on a trial basis. She had never known how to thank him for that, and so she merely put up with him as a way of showing her gratitude.

She had just turned eighteen back then and she had stayed in the job for the following eight years out of loyalty, habit, and a feeling that there was no other job out there for her.

She sighed as she placed another book on the shelf. What was she qualified to do? Other bookshops were run a lot more professionally than Darren's Book Nook. Her quick foray into wanted-ads told her that they would demand that she "showed initiative" and "managed her own workload." She was sure she wasn't ready for that. She figured that a trained monkey could do the job she was doing right now and so that was what she would stick with, no matter how much it bored her.

The little bell above the door rang out. Before Zoe had time to turn to see who their new customer was, she heard Darren's sharp intake of breath. She knew immediately who must be at the door. Rebecca Clare.

Their favourite customer was shaking drops of

water from her elegant brown coat and looked unfairly beautiful despite her red hair being wet and her glasses covered in little raindrops. Zoe stole as many glances as she dared while Rebecca rid herself of the worst of the rain. She admired the fancy high-heeled shoes, the black stockings, and what she could see of the knee-length black dress under her coat. And that was saying nothing about her face; those stunning eyes and the heart-shaped lips were truly mesmerizing. Especially this close up. Rebecca was near enough for Zoe to be able to reach out and brush her cheek. Not that she was daydreaming about that, of course.

Zoe knew she shouldn't be staring. Not only because it was rude, and borderline objectifying, but because Rebecca was way out of her league. And far too old for her. Zoe didn't know how old Rebecca was but she was certainly older than her own twenty-six years. Oh, and to make Rebecca even more of an impossible choice, she was Darren's huge crush too.

Just as Zoe was dragging her gaze away, she saw Rebecca quickly remove her drenched glasses. The water that had rested on them shot out in Zoe's direction, some hitting the side of her face.

Rebecca looked mortified. "Oh, I'm so sorry. Are you all right, there?"

"Yeah, sure! I'm, uh, waterproof," Zoe replied. She hoped her tone was light and jokey but worried that she sounded as terrified as she always felt when this woman spoke to her.

They had never had any long conversations, she realised. Zoe, and by extension, Darren, only knew Rebecca's name because she had ordered books and they always took contact information to be able to call or e-mail the customer when their book arrived.

Rebecca Clare, RebeccaClare@acacia-recruitment.com, Zoe repeated in her head, stopping herself before she reeled off the memorized phone number too.

The contact information, which showed that she must work in recruitment considering the company's name, and Rebecca's fondness for crime-fiction was all Zoe knew about this woman. Well, that and the fact that she had the sort of presence that you couldn't miss. Despite Rebecca's feminine looks and apparel, there was almost a masculine air to her behaviour. Zoe realised that what she saw as masculine could probably be boiled down to confidence, calm, directness, and a sense of power. Rebecca was polite and friendly but in a way that spoke of a person who you couldn't take for granted.

Either way, Rebecca Clare demanded all the attention of her onlookers without having to fight for it. And that, combined with her obvious beauty, took Zoe's breath away. Just as it was doing right now as she stood with droplets of water running down her cheek and Rebecca smiling politely at her.

Zoe wiped away the water from her face with her sweater sleeve and watched Rebecca dry her glasses on a tissue she had taken out of her pocket. Then she put the glasses back on. Zoe struggled to find something to say. Something normal. Something witty.

She heard Darren clear his throat and come rushing over.

"Mrs. Clare, isn't it? Come to pick up your latest bloodcurdling chiller?" He grinned at Rebecca. Zoe realised that he probably thought it was a charming smirk. It wasn't.

"It's *Ms.* Clare," Rebecca replied casually. "And yes, please. I got an email a few days ago and haven't had time to pop in until today."

"Terrible weather for it, though. You should have waited until tomorrow," Darren said, his strange smile still fixed in place.

Zoe saw Rebecca raise an eyebrow for a brief moment.

"Well, it's meant to rain all week, so planning to only go out when it's dry seems futile. We're Londoners, right? We're experts at dealing with rain."

Darren laughed, far too loudly and for far too long. Zoe wondered if Rebecca was suffering from second-hand embarrassment as much as she was right now. Deciding to rescue the other woman, Zoe put the books down and went behind the counter to pick up the book Rebecca had ordered and put it through the till.

When she was done, she handed Rebecca the thick tome. "Here's your book. I've never heard of this author. Is she any good?"

"Very good. Or, at least, her last three books have been. Here's hoping her latest doesn't disappoint." Rebecca looked down at the book and gave the front cover a quick pat. Then she looked back up at Zoe, with a smile.

Zoe felt herself freeze. She was meant to be telling Rebecca the total for the book, and asking if she wanted a bag but all she could do was stare. The charming smile was bad enough but Zoe had just ignored her own advice – never look this woman in the eye.

Rebecca Clare's eyes were a common blue-green colour, but what made them so dangerous was that they always seemed to glimmer. As if Rebecca was constantly happy. Or constantly flirting. It was insanely distracting and Zoe had to force herself to ignore those gorgeous eyes and just say the total sum. She barely remembered to offer a bag for the book.

When Rebecca had paid and thanked her, she turned on her high heels and click-clacked back out into the rain and out of Zoe's line of vision. Zoe sighed deeply and stopped herself when she realised that Darren could probably hear her.

It turned out that she didn't need to worry about that. Darren was busy staring after Rebecca, looking like an abandoned puppy. Zoe looked around at the shop which suddenly looked ten times duller and knew how he felt.

Published by Heartsome Publishing
Staffordshire
United Kingdom
www.heartsomebooks.com

First Heartsome edition: August 2019